THE MISSION

OF

MILDRED

BUDGE

Short stories about church life in the South

Daphne Simpkins

Cover designed by Guin Nance

The Mission of Mildred Budge by Daphne Simpkins
Imprint: Quotidian Books

Printed in the United States of America

First Printing: February 2018
Imprint: Quotidian Books

ISBN-13 978-1-7320158-0-7

For the children
Jon Michael Linna and Roxanne Nicole Linna

"Every day is a good day."
—MILDRED BUDGE

CONTENTS

WHAT I NEVER TOLD THE PREACHER

It's a long way from the pulpit to the pew, and sometimes there's a chasm of silence that exists between the preacher and a church lady. Oh, we talk to him. We shake the preacher's hand on Sunday mornings. We pray for him. We brag about him to others who don't go to our church. But we don't tell the preacher everything. We tell God everything, but we don't tell the preacher.

I think that's fine. I'm not a big believer in sharing your private life with people who don't need to hear it, and the preacher has never really needed to hear my private story. But it exists, as do the stories of church ladies who move about almost invisibly, the way the aged do later in life--slowly and often unseen and unheard.

Sometimes that unheard status is a kind of holy silence where private lives grow honestly and authentically before the Lord. Sometimes that silence represents a reserve. A sanctified surrendering of will can be mistakenly judged as apathy, but sometimes it is just a form of self-defense, too. It is risky and frightening to be known too well in all your non-glory moments. But when the desire of your heart every day of your life is to love and honor God above all others first and to love others well, sometimes you need to break that silence—risk being known by telling some stories.

What follows are some stories about church life and specifically the work of missions—the Grand Commission (a.k.a. as the Great Commission, but I like Grand better). These tales represent some of the back stories of church life that happen to church ladies, and they represent some of what I never told the preacher.

It's not all of it—just enough trouble and truth for today.

Daphne Simpkins
Montgomery, AL 2018

1
PULLING A MARTIN LUTHER

"I was reading Martin Luther's memoir," Mildred said.

"Why?" Fran asked, naturally.

"I don't remember how I came to be reading it," Mildred confessed, brow furrowing.

"Are you sure that's what you were reading? Did Luther write his memoir?" Fran interrupted. Her hair had been freshly done, styled in the tradition of Doris Day but was an enhanced grey, not blond, like Doris'.

"I think it was some kind of sermon, but what I was reading felt like Luther's memoir," Mildred replied. She pushed her brown plastic glasses up on her nose.

Fran stared up at the ceiling, scratching her chin the way her first husband had but her second husband-to-be didn't. Speaking ruminatively, Fran asked, "Do you think sermons are preachers' memoirs?"

"Yes. Many of them are," Mildred replied easily. "Sometimes a sermon is a memoir of a preacher's spiritual growth."

"Don't ever tell a preacher that," Fran warned, unnecessarily. Her blue eyes blazed with conviction. Silence was a church lady's strong suit, especially in the South. Seasoned church ladies did not give up the power of keeping their own counsel inside a deep and holy silence without calculating the risk or the cost.

"Oh, I wouldn't. Certainly not!" Mildred replied emphatically. It was an unnecessary proclamation. Neither church lady ever told any preacher very much.

Fran nodded, comforted, for it is in the small ways that people agree with one another which creates that bond called friendship. Fran and Mildred had been agreeing with one another for years.

"So, you were reading Martin Luther?" Fran prompted, steering Mildred back to her original point. "And....?"

"Bless his heart. Martin Luther said, 'I didn't have much to do with the Reformation. I was having a beer while the Word did the work.'"

Fran grinned at this unexpected report about the Father of the Reformation, an event in world and church history that had just celebrated its 500th anniversary.

"Did Luther really say that? The part about drinking a beer while the Word did the work?"

"Oh, yes, Martin Luther drank beer. His wife Katharina made it," Mildred said. "It was very good beer, or at least his friends thought so. Those two always had a lot of company after they got married. I don't know how she learned the beer recipe. Katharina was a former nun, and I just can't imagine a lot of nuns drinking beer."

"I can," Fran replied instantly. She was a teetotaler, but she understood why others needed or wanted a drink. "Why hasn't some preacher mentioned that little tidbit about the beer in his sermon-ish memoirs from the pulpit? There are a lot of people who would be as interested in Martin Luther having a cold beer as they are those 95 theses suggesting reforms within the church that old monk so famously posted on the church door."

"I don't think Luther's beer was very cold. They didn't have refrigeration back then," Mildred replied, practically. She fiddled with a Band-Aid applied to her right forefinger to protect a series of unfortunate paper cuts that she had acquired after a feverish morning's quest spent paging through cookbooks looking for a wedding cake recipe she could almost remember. Mildred didn't recall which cookbook it was in or the name of the wedding cake, but she thought if she could read the ingredients or see a picture of it, she would recognize it.

"Imagine what it must have felt like to write out 95 reasons to reform the way you worship God in a formal church. Have you ever wanted to write out some messages—the stuff you never say from the pew while the preacher is talking-- and slip over in the dead of night and post your comments on the church door like Luther did?" Fran asked.

Mildred did not answer immediately.

It had been a little over a year since Mildred Budge had stopped grading students' papers and a funny thing had happened to her. She didn't want to grade anyone's papers ever again and that meant she didn't really want to write any kind of reformation suggestion on the church house door. Mildred Budge was content. But she was a friend of Fran's so she maintained a friendly interest in the question. "Other than an occasional suggestion about how to raise money for missions I don't want to pull a Martin Luther at church," Mildred replied honestly. "What would you write, Fran?"

Fran answered immediately. "Put up a handicapped ramp at the front door of the church building so that people with mobility issues can enter the sanctuary the way they could when they were younger and more able. Don't tell me again that we've already got a ramp at the back of the building that is adequate. It's too far to walk. I don't care about the aesthetics of the front of the building being protected either. What I do care about is that moment when you cross the front door threshold into the sanctuary and experience the peace of God. Vespers at twilight!" Fran breathed in wonder. "There's nothing else on earth like the twilight service on a Sunday evening after a good nap. Week after week it's like falling in love over and over again.

"You can't get that feeling just anywhere. You cross that threshold into the sanctuary, and all of a sudden you feel whole. That's when you understand--or remember --what the gospel brings to your life. I want everyone to have that— to have that crossing the threshold experience of remembering wholeness when they enter the sanctuary.

"If kinfolk and caregivers are pushing people in wheelchairs up the long back hallway trying to breathe while hoping their legs won't give out, they don't get that threshold experience," Fran declared flatly. "I want everybody to have that experience of God's welcome. I'd write that down and post it on the church door in a heartbeat—day or night."

Mildred eyed her feisty friend. This was the first time in their years' long friendship that Fran had revealed what it was like for her to enter the sanctuary of the church. Mildred marveled at the confession for it was different from how Mildred crossed the threshold into the sanctuary on Sunday evening. Mildred thought of the times she had crossed over— gone through--and how she had always been aware of the shift from the outside light to that first experience of shadows in the foyer and then looking up and toward the pulpit and the bright lights inside and the lit-up shining faces of her friends—so many friends! But first there were the deacons holding the doors open for her and handing out the Order of Worship bulletin, and sometimes one of the deacons patted her on the shoulder. Mildred always liked those pats on the shoulder. A hello-pat on the shoulder from a welcoming deacon was very warming indeed.

"What else would you write?" Mildred asked, intrigued by her friend's convictions about the unending delights of the gospel.

Fran answered thoughtfully. "I don't want to write down anything else—just that one thing about access to the wonders of evening vespers because it's real important. If they could hear me about that, then I think it would lead them to discover for themselves the other issues that possibly need to be resolved and maybe not. I've lived long enough to know I've been wrong more often than I've been right and that wisdom is sometimes just doing and saying nothing. Sometimes preachers call our silence apathy, but that's not what it is. When you're silent it's mostly because you have lived long enough to know you could be wrong. What would you really write, Millie?" Fran coaxed.

Even between the two old friends there was a reserve, a holding back from time to time.

'God be merciful to me a sinner,' Mildred thought. It was often her first thought about most questions regarding complaint or reform.

Then, Mildred considered writing an invitation to anyone going by the church: 'Come, everyone who thirsts, come to the waters.....' But a lot of people who had never crossed the threshold didn't know they were thirsty. She dismissed the idea.

Instead, Mildred said, "If I actually got around to writing anything, I think I would like to write the preacher a thank-you note. He works awfully hard. I see him working so very hard."

"I see him working hard too. And the elders and the deacons. I don't think they'd appreciate us thumb-tacking thank-you notes to the front door."

"I don't send thank-you notes to the men in the church anyway—just other church ladies. If I want a man to know something, I usually just tell his wife. Wives know how to pass along a message more effectively than posting it on a front door."

"Do you think that men at church ever try to pass along ideas to women in the church through someone else?" Fran asked. "We widows and single women would have a hard time hearing a message from anyone, because we don't have anyone through whom the idea could be passed."

"If they tried to send me a message, I didn't get it," Mildred stated plainly.

"Me neither. Never gotten a message from a man at church in my life either. Just the preaching, which is quite a lot."

"Do you ever wonder what a church man today would write on a piece of paper and nail on the front door of the church in the dead of night? Is there anything a church man wants to say to the church leaders that he doesn't feel able to say out loud in a general meeting?"

Fran thought about the question and shook her head. "I don't know, and for all of the times when you and I have discussed the boundaries of speech and service at church according to gender, the Bible, and traditions that question and my answer that I don't know any more about what church men are really thinking than they know what church ladies are thinking says more about me than I expected to suddenly learn about myself at my age.

2
THE GOLDEN RULE OF MISSIONS

"I have a new idea for raising money for missions," Mildred announced with excitement. She was standing in the kitchen, the sunlight so bright upon her shining in from the window that Fran couldn't see her best friend's face.

"It will work like a dream!" Mildred promised.

"Déjà vu," Fran whispered to Jesus before fixing her face into the kind of pleasant '*Let me hear your idea*' expression that Mildred Budge counted on when she started another conversation about missions at church. Mildred's best friend Fran had many expressions that showed up on her face and which were now etched in furrows and crevices that she did not try to disguise with powder or creams. In that moment, Fran Applewhite adopted the signature expression her grandpappy had worn when he taught Sunday School: pensive and kind. "You have a lot of new ideas about raising money for missions, but they are not always practical," Fran said firmly but kindly.

"This one is," Mildred boasted. "It is one of those golden moments when time and mission meet the here and now."

Fran shook her head. Well-sprayed grey curls stayed firm, attesting to a kind of resilience and persistence often assigned to soldiers standing post. In a way, she was. "What have you been drinking?"

"Just a Coke. Not a whole one. You know I am not supposed to drink Coke."

Mildred had diagnosed Coke as a digestive issue many years ago. She now thought of herself as fasting from Coke, but she drank it rather often. When she did, the caffeine with sugar could cause Mildred Budge to reach a fever pitch of excitement. Fran nodded tolerantly and sat back in her chair and asked, "You want to raise money for missions how—this time?"

"Well, we live in the South, and everyone here still talks about the Civil War...."

"It was the War of Northern Aggression. Surely you have lived in the Cradle of the Confederacy long enough to remember the distinction true Southerners make about our history. Ask Anne Henry. She'll explain it to you."

Anne Henry was the local expert on the Great Waarh and a formidable tennis player. She had the best smile at church but was most famous for not complaining--ever. If you asked her how she was, Anne Henry always said, with zest, "Fine! Fine!"

"I know they have different names for the Waarh," Mildred continued blithely, innocently, too old really to be as naïve as she was about most everything Southern. "But what I mean is that people still like that movie *Gone With the Wind*, and this is where I am going with my idea."

"You have been watching *Gone With the Wind*? Who has time to watch a movie that long anymore?" Fran asked, peering over Mildred's shoulder out the window where life was happening and where people who did not know that real life was found in the vital living presence of the risen Savior of the world walked around like zombies—unconscious zombies. Fran wondered idly if the current cinematic obsession with zombies was some kind of Jungian expression of the collective unconscious and the unconsciously lost who didn't know they were dead in their darkness and were walking fast and going nowhere real because they couldn't see themselves clearly or where they were going without the Light. Fran said none of this to Mildred, whose face was lit up with wonder and hope. Fran loved that about her friend and returned her attention from her post-Jungian theory about zombies to Mildred Budge, who was such an optimist—at her age!

"No. I didn't watch the whole movie. But it was playing on Turner Classic Movies, and I caught a glimpse of that scene where Melanie and Scarlett are at a dance, and they are helping to raise money for the Cause."

"I don't recall any scene in that movie where Scarlett O'Hara raised money for missions. I believe she had other priorities. Ashley Wilkes? Rhett Butler? Saving Tara?" Fran did not add that she had read somewhere that Clark Gable, who played the dashing rogue Rhett Butler, was a good kisser. *'Who was that actress in that movie who said that kissing Clark Gable for the first time made her feel weak-kneed?'* Fran, who understood the wily ways of the flesh, experienced a momentary mental excursion wherein she imagined kissing Clark Gable until her knees went weak, and then realizing that the fancy led to danger, came to her senses, did what Christians call, repent, and with will, discipline, and focus, returned her attention to the conversation about the God-appointed work of any and every Christian: missions.

Mildred was aware that her friend's attention had momentarily split, waited patiently for her to return, and when she did, said: "No, Scarlettt didn't raise money for missions. It was for the Cause, the South!" Mildred clarified. "Frannie, you aren't following me. What are you thinking about?"

"To be perfectly honest I was thinking about what it would be like to kiss Clark Gable," said Fran, who had a fiancé named Winston and who, upon more than one occasion, had kissed Fran enough to cause her to experience weak knees and smudge the lipstick she wore. It was a shade of lipstick ironically called Wine With Everything, and Fran was a 90% teetotaler. There were rare occasions when the abstemious Southern belle would for friendship's sake take a sip of pink champagne at the wedding anniversaries of people who had been married for fifty years or longer. But that was the sum total of Fran's relationship with alcohol.

"I've never thought about that," Mildred replied, wide-eyed. "Kissing Clark Gable." She and Fran had been friends for eons—long enough to say "yes" in public to cashiers at grocery stores and restaurants who asked, "Are you two girls sisters?" and had grown comfortable saying, "Yes, yes, we are," and were not lying. For inside the living love of Jesus they were sisters through and through. Only occasionally one sister wanted to talk about raising money for missions and the other sister wanted to talk about kissing Clark Gable.

"I can live without Clark Gable's moustache," Mildred replied frankly. "Did you know Clark Gable tried out for the part of Tarzan in the early movies and lost out to Johnny Weissmuller?"

"Why would you tell me something like that? You know how I feel about Clark Gable."

"If Clark Gable had become Tarzan he would have swung through trees wearing only a loin cloth, but he didn't look good enough. That's what they said. When he was up for the part, they asked him to take off his shirt, and when he did he lost the part just like that," Mildred said, snapping her fingers, as if she had been there and seen it happen. But she had only read about it

"You had to say that out loud to me?"

"True is true," Mildred said.

Fran shrugged, her hands going up in a move that was meant to be an emulation of a French woman's world weary shrug about kisses and love and 'I give up being wise; just go ahead and pour me another glass of pink champagne, why don't you?'

"You were saying about missions?" Fran prompted. She returned her attention to her friend for they had been sisters long enough to pay one another the persevering courtesy of considering the other's preoccupations whether they shared apprehension about moustaches or not.

It was Mildred's turn to try and emulate a world weary shrug, but she was too excited to be able to do it with the same aplomb that Fran mustered. "Do you recall in the movie when the South needed money to support the troops and someone goes around collecting the women's jewelry and Melanie and Scarlettt throw in their wedding rings to help fund the South's war efforts against that Northern Aggression?"

Fran nodded almost imperceptibly. She wasn't sure, but she was willing to go along with the stated memory. It was easier than watching *Gone With the Wind* again. "What happened at the dance? Was that where Scarlettt couldn't keep her feet still?"

"Yes."

"There's a lot of that nervous energy going around," Fran observed dryly.

Mildred brushed aside the comment. "Why can't we have a gold jewelry collection here? A lot of women have gold jewelry they don't like or want to wear, and there's a terrific market for gold these days. We could raise a lot of money for missions in one day of collecting gold jewelry women aren't even wearing and turn it into cash."

Fran was all attention, her head shaking before she answered flatly, "The missionsman won't go for it. The moneyman won't like it either, and I haven't even gotten to preacherman, but he really won't go for it."

"How do you know that?" Mildred asked, not surprised that Fran was attempting to put the quietus on her suggestion. Fran often scotched Mildred's best ideas.

"The concept is too hard to explain. It's got more than three points to make, and you know preachers are trained in seminary to stick with three points about everything they want to discuss. You have to ask for money fast—preferably in one sentence. It's like the Golden Rule of Missions. The idea has got to hit people right in the old bread basket—the gut!" Fran explained, patting her midriff. She was a petite woman, barely weighing a hundred and ten pounds, but given the opportunity she could eat like a hungry sailor. "If the explanation requires more than one sentence and can't be explained in three easy-to-digest points, it's bound not to work. That's one of the reasons that the Faith Promise campaign is losing ground. It takes too many sentences to explain. If it isn't broke, don't fix it, Mildred," Fran cautioned.

"Huh?" Mildred asked. Clichés offered to her as wisdom never seemed to fit the situation she was in, and her very best friend—her very best sister-friend—often didn't agree with her about her biggest and best ideas for raising money for missions.

"Cold hard cash, honey. Our missionsman needs dough to fund outreach efforts in the name of Jesus--not jewelry that he has to fool with."

"We could fool with it. I could take it to one of those places that buys gold and bring the greenbacks to him."

"Now, see. Right there you have another goofball idea. They aren't going to let you go off with a few pieces of jewelry—and it won't be many-- and come back solo with the moolah."

17

"You'd be with me, wouldn't you? I wouldn't be traveling solo...." Mildred stammered briefly, trying to enter into Fran's rhythm. "With the moolah."

"You don't really know what good stuff is. To you, good-stuff jewelry is anything you bought at its regular retail price. That's not the good stuff. That's costume jewelry just priced high. The good stuff would be worth a lot of money because it's real gold, and the people who might consider giving it would want the good stuff appraised. Then, they would want a receipt so that they could claim a tax deduction."

"Why can't people just toss in some jewelry they don't wear anymore and let the rest of that worry go?"

"Documentation. I don't think the IRS will accept the hearsay evidence of "I threw some jewelry into the plate at church for missions just like Melanie and Scarlett did in the movie *Gone With the Wind* for the Cause."

"You are making too big a deal out of what could or might not happen. It's a simple idea and a good one—like cleaning out a closet except it would be a jewelry box. People have yard sales to raise money for missions. This is kind of like that, only we are cleaning out jewelry boxes. People don't expect to be given receipts from garage sales hosted for missions."

Fran shook her head sadly, trying for a different approach to explain to her friend what Mildred could not seem to grasp. "What's in your jewelry box, Millie?"

"I personally don't have any good jewelry, but other people do," Mildred confessed easily. She rarely thought about jewelry unless she saw it on other people, and then she thought in a kind of passing way, 'That's pretty.' But she never wanted it for herself except from time to time something glittery like a pair of diamond-chip earrings from Costco that she had tried to talk herself into buying until the young man who was managing the display case that day she had asked to see them refused to show the earrings to her. He shook his head, and said with unapologetic conviction, "Oh, no, ma'am. Those earrings aren't for you. They look like something Dolly Parton would wear." And because she was dumbfounded by such a comment and because she had always liked how Dolly Parton looked—so festive, like a party unto herself!-- Mildred Budge had murmured incongruously, "Thank you so much" and walked away from the good stuff in the Costco jewelry counter. But she still thought about those diamond-chip earrings ($119 plus tax) from time to time, especially when Dolly Parton came on the radio.

"And that's your biggest problem right there, Millie. You are asking people to do what you cannot do. The first rule of leadership is that you have to lead or inspire by example. Do you remember how Scarlett tossed in her wedding ring? Her marriage didn't matter to her so it wasn't much of a sacrifice. You have an idea that will cost others a sacrifice, but it won't cost you a thing because you don't have any good jewelry to toss into the collection plate."

"Is that how people think really?" Mildred asked in wonder.

Fran sighed. "You go think about raising money for missions some more, Millie. I have heard about people collecting aluminum cans for the recycling money. You could do that. Lots of people drink beverages out of cans, although I have heard some troubling reports lately about cans not being

19

as safe to eat or drink from as one would hope. I am going to have to read some more about that one day. I seem to have enough to worry about today," she added, fighting the urge to stare out the window. Some more zombies were walking by. All this talk about money for missions in order to send people to help other people abroad when there were so many zombies walking around nearby worried Fran that day and in that moment.

"I don't drink Cokes out of cans," Mildred replied honestly, following Fran's gaze.

"Not the point. Other people do, and other people mostly throw cans away. You could sponsor a recycling project for cans and sell the cans for money for missions."

"Wouldn't the same principle apply? It would cost them their cans but not me because I don't have any. I don't drink Cokes from cans."

Fran appeared to think about it and then said without a qualm, "No. I think people would do that. I really do."

3
LUNCH WITH THE BOYS

When it was Streeter's turn to provide lunch for the Fishes & Loaves Committee, he brought a sack full of foot-long Subway sandwiches and a picnic-sized bag of potato chips that committee members could help themselves to by the fistful and deposit on a spread-out thick white paper napkin on the table top in front of them because there weren't any plates in the conference room where they were meeting.

Eating off a napkin was one of the efficient ways that church lady Mildred Budge ate by herself at home when she didn't want to wash dishes.

"Whaddya want to drink, Millie?" Streeter asked, jiggling some coins in his pocket to signal *I'm buying.* There was a vending machine nearby.

There was no offer of 'Unsweet this or that'-- no crystal pitcher of ice water with lemon wedges.

Mildred replied instantly, honestly, "Coke, please!"

"Coming up," Streeter promised as he walked away and down the hallway of the sprawling Baptist church where they were meeting today—his home church. The Fishes & Loaves committee, which served the homeless and hungry in the city, rotated around to the different churches that had an investment in the multi-denominational mission's ministry and a representative on the governing committee. The rule of the working lunch was simple: when it was your turn to host the meeting, you provided vittles and drinks.

Mildred smiled broadly as the other members—all men-- arrived and saw the ample sandwich sections laid out on the paper sacks which had been torn apart and placed as a surrogate table cloth in the middle of the conference room's table next to the hefty stack of all-purpose white paper napkins.

"Grab a napkin and a sandwich," Streeter directed, as he returned with drinks for everyone. He placed them on the table with an easy nod: *Help yourself.*

There was not a gold-trimmed platter in sight—not a doily nor a decorative garnish. Lunch with the boys was so different from the ladies' lunches and which ladies planned so carefully.

Mildred had sat in front of Anne Henry last Sunday night while she had discussed with Lucy, her co-hostess, the menu of a future ladies' luncheon. "Do we want a thinly-sliced turkey breast with Sister Schubert yeast rolls or Pepperidge Farm party-style bread slices?"

Mildred Budge knew the size of the Pepperidge Farm party-style bread slices. It took four slices to make one regular size piece of bread. It was awfully difficult to take and stack eight small pieces of bread to make four small sandwiches in front of other ladies and not appear to be gluttonous. The yeast rolls were just as small. It didn't matter how hungry you were. Two rolls was the maximum number of rolls any lady could take to make a tiny finger-food sandwich. That's what ladies often called their entrees at luncheons: finger-foods.

Mildred had tuned out the discussion between Anne Henry and Lucy about bread slices and rolls before the final decisions had been made for the luncheon. Whatever was decided, the portions would be petite, and the dessert would most likely be tiny pick-up bites of sweets that ladies ate carefully without touching their lips to the surface in order not to mar their lipstick. Often, dessert was brownies or lemon squares not dusted in powdered sugar because no woman who had experienced the mess of white Confectioner's sugar getting all over her bosom in public dared to inflict that danger or temptation on a well-behaved, well-dressed sister, particularly a well-endowed one.

Mildred often skipped the unsugared lemon squares at ladies' luncheons. *Why spend your calories on that?* It was better to go home and eat a bowl of ice cream and pray for people who didn't know how to accept the rightful inheritance of the saints, which was, in part, what dessert was supposed to be, she believed.

And the church lady believed more than that.

Mildred Budge believed whole heartedly in the second law of loving other people as yourself by actively housing the homeless and feeding the hungry. She fed herself with the bread and water from the Bible, fascinated and flummoxed at the same time by the inscrutable beauty of God's love found throughout the story of his love affair with mankind. Daily Mildred Budge opened the Bible and asked the Master of the Feast of Life: *"What do you mean by that? And that? Feed me lots and lots of manna! No bite-sized pieces of bread, please! I want lots—full-sized pieces of bread! Drench me in Living Water!"*

And she always prayed for people who didn't relish dessert and for people who trimmed their azalea bushes into perfect squares. They cut off perfectly beautiful flowers to create a square bush. Bushes like that filled Mildred with dismay—the same kind of dismay that she felt for people who didn't understand why dessert mattered. Dessert was always something one should be able to look forward to! So were flowers in the spring on gently snipped bushes!

As if reading her mind, Streeter suddenly extracted a big bag of M & M's, tore it open, laid it within arm's reach, and announced, "Grab some dessert."

"Merciful Jesus," Mildred breathed, a blessing of sorts.

Sandwiches were consumed, chips chewed, drinks drunk, and prayers spoken as decisions were made and money spent to help the less fortunate of God's children. During the meeting, men laughed a lot and ribbed each other in a way that reminded Mildred of how fifth grade boys on the playground batted a ball around among themselves without fear of hurting one another. If someone did get slammed by a veering ball— or at the meeting, a roughly spoken comment—the other guy ignored it or slammed it jokingly right back at him.

At lunch with the boys, no one got his feelings hurt.

By meeting's end, Mildred was thinking she would just provide the same sumptuous manly, practical sandwich meal when it was her turn to host the Fishes & Loaves committee at her home church.   There would be no covered basket with tidy crust-less sandwiches, no peach-flavored artificially sweetened ice tea, and no tiny desserts naked of Confectioner's sugar. Instead there would be this: fist-sized fat sandwiches with lots of meat and veggies, salty chips, a variety of icy cold, sugary drinks, and colorful M & M's lavishly poured onto the multi-purposed paper napkin from which everyone just grabbed some and popped them unselfconsciously—it looked like gluttony, but it was really a healthy appetite!-- into their mouths. Mildred liked the red ones best.   She was just about to blot her lips on her well-used paper napkin when it occurred to her that something had happened at this lunch with the boys that didn't happen at ladies lunches, ever: she was full.

4

WIDOW'S MITE NITE

"So, how it would work is that we'd explain the event in the church bulletin as Widow's Mite Nite, and we'd serve pita pockets as the fellowship supper entree. After everyone fills their pita pockets with grilled chicken nuggets, lettuce, and tomatoes, they can empty their pockets and purses for missions in a container we'll call the Widow's Mite treasury."

Exhilarated by her inspiration to raise money for missions, Mildred Budge waited expectantly for her best friend Fran to applaud—at least this once—her newest idea.

A famous realist, Fran didn't. "Nobody will go for it, because they will think giving on Widow's Mite Nite would stop people from filling out the Faith Promise pledge card. That event is coming up!"

Faith Promise was the annual pledge campaign to raise support for missions. Ideally, one was supposed prayerfully to write down a dollar amount and then trust God to supply that money for missions. Enthusiasm was wavering. It was time for a change. At least Mildred Budge thought so. She tried to always sound optimistic and positive about Faith Promise; but deep down, down where she kept her deepest secrets, Mildred Budge thought her church had outgrown the strategic theme of Faith Promise. That giving strategy had outlived its purpose. It was like training wheels on a bicycle. You need them while you are learning to ride—to give and why you do it-- but once you know how to keep your balance and are sure of the direction toward which you are going, you don't need the Faith Promise training wheels anymore to give. You make a decision, make a budget, and then give sacrificially rather than out of a windfall.

"This isn't an either/or situation. It's a this-plus-that opportunity. People will still give to Faith Promise, and they will give to this, too. It's a simple plan. They can bring as much cash or change as they want to—or can afford to give on the spot-- but this is not in lieu of Faith Promise. Giving during Widow's Mite Nite for missions is in addition to Faith Promise," Mildred stressed. Mildred Budge was a dedicated team player—really.

Mildred's brown eyes were lit up with a kind of zeal that worried Fran. There were times when Mildred Budge appeared to be becoming a religious zealot or just a real Christian. It was difficult to know when someone had become herself inside a spiritual calling or had simply gone over the edge of reason into a domino-falling dynamic of one feverish thing leading to another.

Fran, church lady of the South, did not say this to Mildred Budge, another church lady of the South, however. Instead her blue eyes warmed with affection and patience, and that

28

response proved what she believed to be true about her friend, a real Christian. "Mildred, most people don't know what a pita pocket is." Fran said as she scratched her chin. "It even sounds kind of fishy: pita pocket-- pick your pocket. And, pita pockets don't even have the appeal of a hot potato. (A Hot Potato bar had only been tried once for fellowship supper night, and no one had requested it again.) The people who come to fellowship suppers don't want a lunch-type meal. They want a dinner-type meal, and a pita pocket is a lunch-type entree."

"That's not the point," Mildred replied immediately, trying hard not to raise her forefinger which she was too often tempted to wave and point when she was speaking animatedly. She had seen herself do that once in the eyes of her best friend Fran Applewhite, and had been trying to censor that hand motion in herself ever since. "Surely by now grown-up people know that fellowship suppers are not about the food; they're about the fellowship. Grown-up Christians can't listen to a thousand sermons on missions and not already believe that whatever your personal views about missions, once your church establishes its plan, you should support that plan and missions to the last mite of your might."

"That's a good slogan right there," Fran said, and she wavered. She would dearly love to be able to support Mildred in one of her fundraising-for-missions plans, but her best friend was famously naïve about the ways of the world and the church. To compound the problem Mildred had a lot of energy for it—a lot of energy. Fran saw it as her duty to keep Mildred out of trouble. Last year Mildred Budge had recklessly proposed a Bon Voyage Party for missionaries headed to foreign fields and had exuberantly suggested that bubbly grape juice be served to keep things jolly. "It's not alcoholic, and it's so festive!"

"We can't do that," Fran had replied, stifling a moan that had for the past three years been just below the surface when she and her best friend talked about missions. "We must avoid even the appearance of evil, and bubbly grape juice served at church looks bad. Bad." Oh, no. Mildred Budge was not good at seeing ahead to the future and around corners. That Bon Voyage party for departing missionaries and serving sparkling grape juice was a disaster waiting to happen.

Mildred had registered Fran's objection and let the idea go, but not because she agreed with her friend. She had abandoned the idea of a Bon Voyage party out of respect for her friend's views about alcohol. When Fran objected, Mildred had not even brought up the Bible verse that recommended using a little wine for the stomach's sake. Fran knew the Bible as well as Mildred, but she also volunteered with hospice. Fran knew from experience that too many people died from alcohol poisoning, and that wasn't the worst of it. After a family member drank himself to death (well, that's what happened!), his kinfolk pressed on with the damages caused by having lived with an alcoholic. Mildred and Fran had discussed the slippery slope of social drinking early in their friendship. Fran had explained: "A little wine for the stomach's sake in a perfect world might be all right; but in a fallen one, drinking can lead to bad health, death, and all kinds of heartbreak. Better not to gamble by drinking hard or soft liquor on a regular basis."

So Mildred had let go of the Bon Voyage party idea, and now she was going to bury her envisioned pita pocket Widow's Mite Nite fund-raising event that Fran didn't like either.

There was a tradition in place for the missions fundraising; and while ideas were always actively sought to refresh and generate enthusiasm, this challenge of giving everything you had on you for missions during a regular fellowship supper night was, apparently, too extreme a proposal. Couple it with pita pockets for a fellowship meal, and according to a realist, the proposal was a no-go from the get-go.

Mildred had recently heard a sermon on running the race set before you, so she tried again. "By now every adult who comes to our fellowship suppers has been tested in love—has discovered what it feels like to lay down their life for someone else. It does something to you-- that kind of extreme giving. You get a taste for it. I read a book by Pearl S. Buck about people in India having a better understanding than we do about that kind of self-giving to the community. I think we should create an environment where it is socially acceptable to be totally giving—to look like a Christian crackpot. I'll be happy to go first-- pour the entire contents of my wallet into the mission's treasury. They can spend it anyway they choose. I need to practice sacrificial giving, and that includes giving up my opinions and agendas."

"You can't do your charitable deeds before others. That's blowing your own trumpet," Fran objected immediately.

"I'm not blowing a trumpet. I'm following the Bible. I'm imitating the generous widow. "

"You've never been married," the realist replied. "How can you exemplify a widow?"

That was a low blow--a very low blow.

A great believer in living peacefully as far as one could, Mildred said, "So, we can only write out a check after we have filled out the blue Faith Promise pledge card?"

"Now you understand giving to missions at church," Fran assented with a raised wave of her right hand—a move she only used when she was absolutely sure she was right. To her credit, Fran did not wave that right hand in just that way very often, and Mildred softened, understanding her widowed friend very well.

"But there can be no wild abandon in giving here in the church, no reckless-here-take-it-all giving for missions just because it could be kind of fun?"

"Fun?" Fran sniffed, and looked toward Mildred's refrigerator. She had seen two pepperoni pita pocket sandwiches prepared in there for their lunch, and she wanted hers. Even as she considered helping herself, Fran warned Mildred, "This whole business about pita pockets could blow up in your face, Mildred. I wouldn't present it to the missionsman."

"I simply don't see how Widow's Mite Nite is a problem. No one has to do it, but people could. I think there would be a lot of laughing and teasing about how broke we all are most of the time. That could be fun to just kind of explain that from time to time we are all a little cash poor. I don't carry as much cash as I used to, but on any given day anyone who wants what I have in my wallet can have it. I would just as soon give it all to a missionary as to a stranger."

Fran eyed the refrigerator. Her stomach rumbled. "What kind of dessert would you serve with a pita pocket sandwich?"

"What if we just fasted from desserts and used the money we saved for missions? There's another idea right there," Mildred said, nodding her head rapidly in hopes that this one time--surely one time!-- her friend could agree with her for old time's sake. For friendship. For fun, even.

Exasperated and hungry, Fran snapped, "Isn't it time for you to rotate off the missions committee? Have you considered the possibility that you're becoming a religious zealot?"

Mildred had considered that--had considered that just possibly she wasn't a religious zealot but obsessive compulsive and that talking missions was an obsession of hers. Tucking the concern away in that part of her brain where she stored the disappointment over not having that Bon Voyage party for missionaries—it still felt like a really good idea to her!— Mildred added quickly a suggestion of a dessert for pita pockets. "Little cups of ice cream. We could serve cups of ice cream for dessert for pita pocket Widow's Mite Nite. Just hand 'em out, no trouble at all."

"Well, now you're talking. What kind of ice cream are you thinking about?"

"I would have suggested Blue Bell but that company has been having a peck of trouble. It has crossed my mind that we could have a fund-raiser to buy the church its own industrial-sized ice cream maker like some restaurants have so patrons can serve themselves. We could have chocolate ice cream on one side and vanilla ice cream on the other. It would boost attendance on fellowship night." Mildred had a lot of ideas about church life, and Fran heard most of them.

"And you can swirl the flavors together?" Fran said, her blue eyes narrowing. She scratched her chin again. "We could have a special fund-raiser for THAT, and any extra money that came in after we bought the ice cream machine could go to missions," Fran suggested.

"You mean we could have Widow's Mite Nite to buy an ice cream machine...."

"Oh, yes," Fran said easily. "People love ice cream."

5
SIBEL, YOU'RE GETTING FAT

"Sibel, you are getting fat!" Mildred heard herself say the words after "hello" and could not stop them from tumbling out. Even as she watched Sibel's mouth shape an "O" followed by a series of rapid eye blinks as if she might suddenly pass out, Mildred continued: "You don't know how heavy you are getting because the weight's creeping up on you. You live alone, and there's no one in your house to take note of what they call in polite society—love handles—and mention it to you. So, you're gaining weight and growing stiff and awkward with yourself and calling that discomfort growing older, but it's not your age alone, Sibel. You're getting fat."

Sibel looked hurriedly around to see who else had heard Mildred Budge begin to have a nervous breakdown that started with this symptom that people might associate with Tourettes Syndrome—that condition where you are liable to say anything that comes to mind, and which, when it happens with older women, they blame on menopause or call dotty.

"Dotty," Sibel said the word solemnly, as if this were Mildred's new name. Then her right hand reached to her left wrist where Sibel took her own pulse. Her heartbeat felt funny: erratic and weak. Sibel cocked her head and looked at her old friend Mildred Budge to see if something more than Tourettes, dementia, or menopause was taking hold of her friend-- something like an alien or a demon who was trying to take over her friend's body. Sibel leaned toward Mildred while her left hand was pressed against the center of her bosom where truth resided—still counting her own heartbeats just in a different location—and stared deeply inside Mildred's large brown eyes. *Yes, it was Mildred Budge.* Still, Sibel hissed the phrase, "Get out of her you demon of discouragement!" Her voice was surprisingly soft for use in an exorcism, so Sibel bravely, with determination, cleared her throat, deepened her voice, and declared, "In the name of Jesus, I cast you out of Mildred Budge, you demon of discouragement."

Mildred did not back away or waver. "The truth is not a demon, Sibel. Besides, demons only come out with prayer and fasting, and you have not been fasting."

As best as Sibel could determine, the living soul was Mildred Budge and so the face and the mouth and the words were Mildred's, or the tailwind of Mildred who was possibly being abducted by aliens and all that was left was this echo of accusation—these words of meanness.

Sibel had a sudden image of that stream of hot air that forms a white trailing cloud behind planes that zoom overhead.

That's what the words looked like to her as they hung in the air between the two church ladies.

You're getting fat. And underneath that and in front of it and behind it was a sure knowledge: Sibel's friend Mildred Budge loved her.

They were longtime friends. True friends. Southern sisters. Jesus girls.

"Fat?" Sibel confirmed solemnly. Dully. A question mark showed up only after the sounding of the word like a gong between them and then the raising of the carefully drawn on eyebrows, the release of the hand from the center of her bosom where she had been pierced with the truth. Her flesh, her hand, her denial could not stop the truth from piercing her heart.

"The way I know about you is because I have gotten fat, too. I only wish someone had had the courage to tell me when I needed to know it a while back. You'd think with as many people who call themselves my friend one of them would have told me that it looked like I was gaining weight. You know how hard it is to see yourself clearly," Mildred stated flatly.

Sibel blinked slowly, the features of her face settling back into the expression she wore when she was out in public and trying to be polite. The light in her sweet blue eyes (that's how people described the color of Sibel's eyes) which had been bright with shock mellowed to a glow that was indicative of tolerance and persevering. This response was an amen of sorts. This sharing of hard truths and outrage and surprise settled down almost immediately. They were friends.

While studying Mildred to see how fat her friend had gotten, Sibel thought instantly of the series of mirrors stationed around her house where she lived alone. There was the mirror over the sink in the bathroom where she checked her teeth after brushing and before leaving the house, the mirror over her dresser in her bedroom she used to make sure she had buttoned her blouse correctly, the standing mirror in its own frame in the spare bedroom where the coats were stored for chilly days and where she checked the reflection of herself in the wintertime to see how the coat was hanging and in the summertime, how her slip was hanging (was it showing?) when she wore a dress, though Sibel didn't wear a slip much anymore because she didn't wear a dress as often as she once did.

Those were Sibel's mirrors and the reasons she used them. She hadn't checked the mirrors to see if she were getting fat since she had stopped weighing on the bathroom scale once the 9-volt battery had died, and that was two years ago. She kept the scale in the dirty clothes hamper now and only noticed it when she pulled out the soiled clothing to take to the washer. For a couple of years she had been telling herself routinely, "You need to buy a 9-volt battery" when she should have been saying, "You need to know if you are gaining weight so buy a 9-volt battery." She had stopped wanting to know because she didn't want to face the truth. That was the truth.

Sibel's left hand moved from the reassuring beat of her settling-down heartbeat to her face, where she felt the thickening tissues. *Yes, it was fuller there. Fatter. Her chin had a slight sag underneath that was truly disheartening.*

She would float easily in water.

Mildred gave her friend time to go through the process she had already experienced at a recent visit to the doctor for a simple annual check-up, which was similar to the stages of grief: anger, denial, and finally, acceptance. "If someone had told me how fat I was getting I might have done something about it before I became this uncomfortable. And now it's not a matter of making simple choices of cutting back on a pat of butter. I have to actually walk four miles a day and not eat ice cream for a long, long time. I can't even have a cup of cocoa at eight o'clock at night until I get down to a slimmer size."

Mildred leaned closer to reveal the final truth that she didn't want anyone other than Sibel to hear: "My doctor told me that I am technically obese."

In spite of her own chagrin, Sibel felt her friend's pain and repeated mournfully, "You are obese. Obese." That sounded much worse.

Mildred's eyes widened. "You will be obese, too, if you don't cut back on eating now. I'm just telling you because I am obese—that means I'm fatter than you are."

And with that, Mildred Budge walked off, her step pretty lively since she had been walking. Her muscles had become more limber and her derriere less than it had been a month before when she had faced the truth. She had gotten fat.

She left behind her friend who had heard her and who said, in a light gasp, "I didn't know. I really didn't know."

6

SPIRITUAL GIFTS: X
MARKS THE SPOT

"Last Wednesday night preacherman gave out one of those forms where we are supposed to mark the boxes next to the gifts of the Spirit that we have...."

"So we can use them in church?" Mildred Budge asked, unnecessarily.

Lucy nodded dismissively. She was wearing a short dark fur jacket over a pair of black flannel pajama bottoms, which she had taken to wearing to evening worship. The design on the pajamas was gold stars and silver crescent moons.

"That form didn't surprise me," Lucy said, crossing her legs unselfconsciously. "What did surprise me," Lucy said, leaning closer while still staring ahead at the vacant podium. (Preacherman hadn't come out yet.) "My spiritual gifts today aren't the same ones I would have checked the box next to twenty years ago. You don't lose spiritual gifts, do you?" Lucy asked Mildred, who had learned her lesson from interrupting the last time and so didn't say anything this time except to shrug and reach into her handbag for a piece of candy, a Honee, her signature throat lozenge.

Mildred held the tube of candy out to Lucy, who shook her head, no. Lucy didn't eat sweets—a point of view so different from Mildred Budge's that it was a wonder they were friends, but they were good friends, actually. Mildred was on a diet and only allowed herself two Honees a day now. Her doctor had told her she was a bit overweight.

"Twenty years ago I marked the box that said I had the gift of encouragement. But I don't know if that's true now. On Wednesday afternoons I volunteer here at the church as the receptionist. When people call and ask me what's on the menu for fellowship supper, I say...." Lucy's tone grew sharp as she imitated the sound of herself on the phone, "Don't you read the church newsletter? It said we are having hot dogs."

Mildred didn't interrupt to add that people called the church about the fellowship supper menu when they knew it was hot dog night hoping somebody had come to their senses and changed the entree because hot dogs are indigestible.

"I tell them to start reading the newsletter that comes in the mail," Lucy reported herself as saying. "In short, when I hear myself answering questions on the telephone at church I often don't sound like I have the gift of encouragement."

"Gift of helps?" Mildred offered tentatively, because, after all, her friend was up at the church volunteering her help; but before she could explain herself, Lucy shook her head definitely, no.

"I can hear myself talking. I'm not much help."

"Well, if everybody has at least one spiritual gift, and you think you don't have the gift of encouragement anymore...." Mildred hesitated. She didn't want to pursue that line of thought because it could lead to nowhere encouraging. Instead, she asked, "Which box did you mark?"

"Giving. I marked the box next to giving. I give and give," Lucy said flatly. "When someone wants something from me, I write them a check and say, 'Now go away and leave me alone.'"

"You marked that box?" Mildred asked. "I didn't see that box. We could all mark that box!" What a relief. Mildred decided right then that the next time preacherman gave a self-evaluation spiritual inventory form to fill out, she would look for that box in order to pass the test of having a socially acceptable spiritual gift. Exhorting and rebuking were never on there.

Lucy nodded affirmatively, watching for the pianist to play the overture to the worship service and for preacherman to emerge from the little room where he readied himself before coming out to give the sermon.

Mildred followed Lucy's expectant gaze. 'A preacher's first step toward the pulpit after days of preparation in meditative solitude and deep prayer must be a difficult one to make each week,' Mildred thought every week before every sermon. 'You've been living inside a prayer before it becomes a sermon, and then you have to share the fruit of that deep prayer that has been forming inside of you all of a sudden with blank, sleepy faces.' Mildred often wanted to call out to preacherman just before he spoke: "We're glad to see you, and we're on your side!" But there was no time during the service for anyone at all to speak to preacherman except to risk an "Amen" from time to time when the moon was blue.

'There was a basic flaw in the format of sermons,' Mildred thought. 'A sermon was one-sided and meant to be two-way engaged, but it was difficult to create a two-way engagement with so much space between you and that wooden pulpit behind which the preacherman stood and which routinely functioned like a small wall.'

"In addition to filling out that form we had another form where we are supposed to sign up for the women's retreat."

The subject of the women's retreat came up every year, as regular as clockwork.

"Did you sign up?" Mildred asked as the piano began its soft entreaty of a call to worship. Peggy was playing. Mildred loved Peggy, who had recently taken to patting her friend Mildred on the head whenever they were talking in the hallway outside the ladies' room. Mildred liked having her head patted by Peggy, and now the same gentle, patting musical hand— both hands—were playing the music that called people to worship. Mildred enjoyed knowing Peggy. Her friend Peggy had the spiritual gift of making you feel loved by patting you on the head. There was no box to mark with an X to say you have the gift of making others feel loved. Peggy had it. Everybody knew it too—no form needed!

"Parts of it. I'm going up for the day, but I'm not going to spend the night. I don't sit around in my pajamas talking to other women."

"You don't?" Mildred asked, incredulous.

"Nope," Lucy said, shaking her head emphatically and recrossing her legs--more gold stars and silver crescent moons on the other leg. "I'm too old for that. I'll go back up for part two the next day. Do you want to go with me? I could pick you up."

The two friends had the same conversation year after year no matter where the retreat was located. Lucy always went. Mildred never did.

"No, I don't like to go to places where people talk a lot," Mildred said.

"You really should go, Mildred. It would be good for you-- bring you out of your shell." Lucy said the same thing pretty much every year.

Every year, Mildred wondered why Lucy thought she needed to come out of her shell. 'What shell was she talking about?'

"Did you hear that?" Mildred asked, as a broad smile crossed her face. "You were being encouraging right then. And before that, when you offered to pick me up, you were being helpful. That's so sweet. Bless your heart."

"I was?" Lucy asked, incredulous. "I was just talking."

"You haven't lost your spiritual gift of encouragement. You just express it differently than you used to because we're older, and we don't have much time left so we don't speak as politely anymore. We cut right to the chase now. You are too encouraging!"

Mildred's response did not encourage Lucy. She grew wistful. "I didn't mark that box though. I should have just marked it for old time's sake. And I do love preacherman. He's so sweet. I would do anything for him really, and I guess if you feel like that about preacherman, you ought to be able to fill out a form and smile at him afterwards."

"They'll probably give you another form to fill out if you ask for it," Mildred suggested. "You could revise it, and you could smile at him then. I smiled at preacherman twice last week."

"Two whole times?"

"Uh-huh. I wasn't sure he saw me the first time, so I smiled at him a second time."

Just that quickly, Lucy's tone grew sharp again. She was a good thinker, and sometimes her thoughts came faster than others expected them to do. "I love the preacher; but if I start smiling at him too much, he might want to come up with some more forms for us all to fill out. I don't want to fill out any more forms. The other day while I was answering the phone they made me sort the forms. I don't like to sort forms any more than I like to fill them out. When I volunteered to answer the phone they didn't tell me I would have to sort forms. I'm thinking about quitting. I'm not as young as I used to be when I first volunteered to be nice up here. So are you going to the retreat at all—for the day at least?"

"No, I never go to the retreats. I really don't like to go to places where you have to do a lot of intimate sharing," Mildred said definitely. "I just go to church."

7

LOOSE CHANGE AND HAPPY DOLLARS

"What if on the fifth Sunday of the month we take up an extra collection of loose change for missions?" Mildred proposed.

Fran didn't respond immediately. Instead, she stared out the window at a red bird and prayed out loud in front of Mildred Budge: "Please make more red birds, Lord. I love red birds."

Instead of saying amen, Fran then returned her attention to Mildred's suggestion about collecting loose change. "Empty out your purse right now," Fran demanded, looking at Mildred with a glance that could only translate: *I dare you.*

Mildred was up to it. Immediately she up-ended her big church lady purse and watched the cache of supplies tumble onto the counter top. It contained the usual stuff: Kleenex, a Tylenol bottle, a small hair brush, three red lipsticks, toothpicks in cellophane, dental floss in the trial size they give you at the dentist, and all kinds of coins. There were pennies, nickels, dimes, oh, and a button—that shiny black button from her good black slacks that had come off in her hand and which she had tossed into her purse to reattach, only she had forgotten. There it was. Mildred reached over and picked up the needed button, a smile of pleasure dawning on her face.

Fran reached over and patted her best friend's hand. "It always surprises you to find the things you put where you will find them so that you won't lose them."

"It does," Mildred agreed, for she heard no criticism in that observation, and there was none intended. "It means I am not losing my mind. I like believing that."

Then, Fran began to separate the loose change, making a small pile of coins on the side of the table.

"Looks like you've got a couple of bucks here," she said. "Enough to buy us each a hamburger for lunch at Burger King if we stick with the Value Menu."

"And that's just what came out of the bottom of my purse," Mildred said, ignoring the prompt. "Watch this," Mildred said, unzipping her wallet. She shook it over the pile of coins and more change fell down.

"Three dollars and counting," Fran quickly calculated.

Mildred grinned, following Fran's finger as she too counted the coins, automatically moving the quarters together, the dimes in a pile, the nickels to one side, and ignoring the pennies. Pennies were a lot of trouble. "Now imagine if every woman in the Berean class just decided to throw in the loose change from her purse on that fifth Sunday of the month. It might come to a hundred dollars or so. If we did that a couple of times throughout the year—how many fifth Sundays are there?"

Fran shrugged.

"If the class agreed we could try it for a year and see how it works out. Should we have a project in mind to give it to or just turn the money in for missions?"

"What will the moneyman think about receiving a bunch of coins that have to be counted and rolled before being deposited in the bank?" Fran asked, though the two friends had discussed this issue many times. The conversation ran the way it usually did with each woman playing her part.

"The moneyman won't like it. That man is accustomed to working with checks and hard cold cash," Mildred said.

"Why don't we buy one of those machines that rolls coins and do the job ourselves? We could roll the coins, turn that into cash, and then give it to him," Fran proposed.

"That makes too much sense, and somehow, it kind of takes away from the excitement of emptying our purses that way and robs us of the fun of watching to see what falls out," Mildred said.

"You always want life to be fun, Mildred—even at church. And it just isn't. Life is about rolling the coins and turning them into cash before turning them into the church so the moneyman won't be mad at us."

"I am losing interest in the idea as I sit here," Mildred said, staring out the window where two red birds now sat in the tree outside her window. Sunlight filtered in through the limbs, landing on the bark, the leaves, the ground, creating shadows and images that an artist would want to turn into a painting.

She was in awe. "I love red birds, too," she said with wonder in her voice.

"It's not the worst idea you've ever had," Fran allowed. "Though I do want you to know that this is a variation on that earlier suggestion you had about Widow's Mite Nite. This is that, kind of--just inside the Berean class instead of church wide. I know what you're up to, Mildred Budge."

"Just thinking out loud."

"That will ultimately be your downfall if you think out loud with anyone other than me."

"This shouldn't worry anybody."

Fran shook her head. "Having too many ideas at church will make you a problem for somebody, and if you start saying things like this—and that Happy Dollar idea you mentioned to me after Anne Henry took you to that Special K meeting-- you will be considered a problem."

"It wasn't a Special K meeting. It was that group that helps to fund the State Fair. They started their meeting calling the roll while a woman named Judy—I love the name Judy--went around the room with a basket asking for happy dollars."

"I remember that part. I never met Judy, but I like her-- liked hearing about her."

"Judy had a very sweet face and a very nice voice, and when people threw a happy dollar into her collection basket, she said, 'I'm so happy you're here.'"

"But they got to say why they're happy first."

"That's right," Mildred affirmed. "It was wonderfully uplifting to find something to be happy about. Like counting your blessings. That happy dollar contribution gave you a reason to remember why you were happy and to share that happiness with others in a symbolic but tangible way."

"And I loved the explanation they gave you for the collection of the happy dollars. For the children."

"For the children. That's what Judy said. And that's all Judy needed to say."

"I wonder if you ought to tell the missionsman that one phrase. It's not even as long as a whole sentence! Because really, 'for the children' is the answer to why we need to fund missions. For the children of God and for the children who haven't come to their senses yet. It has a nice ring to it." Fran stopped for a moment and played with the possible sentences in her mind, wondering if they could be merged into one sentence that fit the Golden Rule for Missions: tell the story of the fund-raising goal and the envisioned results in one sentence or expect the idea to be a dud.

"Happy dollars for the children," Mildred said, testing it.

"And still you come up with this business about humiliating the whole class of Bereans by expecting them to empty their purses out in front of one another on the fifth Sunday."

"We could have a trash can nearby and throw out all the stuff that accumulates," Mildred suggested.

"The ladies would not want to display the trash they tote around with all the loose change," Fran explained.

"I don't have that much pride," Mildred said.

"That's actually the right kind of pride to have, Millie. You should have that kind of pride. It's called human dignity."

"I've never been able to distinguish between the right and wrong kind of pride and human dignity. When I die, I hope they don't give me a very dignified funeral service. I'd rather people had fun. I've been thinking about telling preacherman exactly that. Don't give me a very dignified funeral."

And as they stared with awe at the red birds the two friends let go of the idea of collecting loose change or happy dollars for missions. Beauty had ahold of them. Beauty. It was powerful. Transfixing. Inspiring. Money hardly seemed worth mentioning in the same sentence as one mentioned a red bird made by God himself for his image-bearers to enjoy.

◆ ◆ ◆

On the next fifth Sunday Fran and Mildred stopped at the back table in the Berean Sunday School room where Fran signed the roll each week to prove that she was present in class that day and which Mildred ignored because she didn't like to fill out forms at church and had decided to stop caring whether people knew if she was in Sunday School or not. There, Fran emptied her purse onto the counter, scooped the coins into the collection basket for missions—their class supported three bona fide missionaries!--and without looking at her friend, promptly sat down. Then, Mildred, who was not surprised that Fran had changed her mind without telling her, emptied her loose change from her purse into the missions' collection basket, and went and sat down wordlessly by her friend.

The next Berean in line, having witnessed this odd phenomenon, assumed that she must have missed out on the details of a new collection plan and automatically emptied the loose change from her wallet into the palm of her hand and then tossed it with her regular contribution of three one dollar bills into the missions' basket.

The lady behind her who was waiting to sign the roll saw the additional contribution of change into the missions' basket and said, "What a good idea. All these coins weigh down my purse, and I've been meaning to toss them into the jar at home. Just keep forgetting." She tossed her coins in and sat down with a smile.

By the time the ladies had filed into class and signed themselves in, collected the prayer sheets, found their hymnals, and arranged themselves next to someone they'd been wanting to visit with since the week before, the idea of taking up a special collection of loose change had begun and no one had even said a word, except Fran, who always seemed to have the last word about these things. She leaned over to Mildred and whispered, "The moneyman isn't going to like us very much after this."

"Let's apologize!" Mildred suggested, as Kathleen began to play a hymn that neither of them could recognize right away. Kathleen was a big fan of arpeggios and often played so many at the beginning of the morning's sing-a-long hymn that you had a hard time hearing the melody until she got to it, and then, oh, boy, you could hear it.

"Beautiful," Fran commented.

"Beauty. It makes you do things and not worry about the things you do."

And then the class began to sing as ladies continued to come in and stop for a moment by the collection basket, now emptying their purses of loose change for missions on the fifth Sunday.

The new class donation system was in place, and there had never been a public discussion or vote about it.

8
RECIPES FROM THE GRAVE

illie B. came up with another one of her ideas the other day in Circle meeting when the floor was open one more time to adopt a fund-raising project.

It usually costs us more to have a fund-raiser than we earn from the activity itself, and I was hoping at first someone would say those words out loud or at least say 'I'll give you a hundred dollars right now if you won't make me go to another banquet,' but that's not what happened.

Millie raised her hand like a school kid does, and why wouldn't she? Millie taught school for a hundred-plus years. She said, "Why don't we put together a cookbook?"

Before the groaning commenced, she stood up and continued, "No, really. I don't think we need another cookbook with recipes we're all still making. I think we could put together a cookbook from recipes our mothers cooked but didn't share with us. It would contain the recipes for the dishes we miss the most."

Well, the room went dead quiet is what happened, because everybody was thinking our Millie was losing it, and her best friend saw that too. Fran stood up right beside Mildred and added her two cents' worth. "Mildred means that we all have some old favorite dish our mother or grandmother used to make. We don't have that recipe now, and that's the very taste of home we want. I know my grandmother made a banana bread in an old cast iron skillet, and I've never been able to duplicate it."

Just as I was logically wondering if you don't have the recipe, how are you going to contribute it to a cookbook, Anne Henry bounced to her feet. She has a hard time sitting still in our Circle meeting, being a tennis champion and all, and she said, real excited although she doesn't like to eat and how she could get truly excited about food is something I don't understand, but who's to say what goes on inside another woman? "My mother didn't enjoy cooking. I don't enjoy cooking much either. But my mama did make an apple salad that was splendiferous, absolutely delectable, and I miss her apple salad especially in the fall when the apples are so good."

"What did it have in it?" Mildred asked with great curiosity.

"It was mostly apples—bite size cubes."

"Diced," Fran clarified.

"I guess that's right. Yes, diced. And it had raisins, and pecans, and small marshmallows, slivers of pineapple, maraschino cherries, and there was a dressing—a creamy white dressing."

"Did the dressing taste lemony?" Fran asked, leaning forward.

The whole room grew quietly expectant, because here was a mystery evolving right in front of us, and the only person in the room who didn't know the solution was the woman who had a taste for....

"Waldorf Salad is what your mother was making," Fran declared.

Anne Henry shook her head. "I know what Waldorf Salad is. Don't you think I've eaten Waldorf Salad? This was something else."

"Did it have whipped cream?" Mildred asked politely.

"Waldorf Salad is made with mayonnaise, and mother's had....maybe. It could have been whipped cream," Anne Henry agreed, startled. Could a mystery that meant so much be solved so easily?

"It was probably whipped cream cut with the juice of half a lemon plus two tablespoons of white sugar," Lucy, the Circle leader, stated rising. "What your mother probably made was the original Supreme Waldorf Salad. You've been eating knock-off Waldorf Salad like the rest of us. These days people eat all kinds of stuff with the same name as what we used to eat, but newer dishes are made with substitute ingredients like mayonnaise instead of whipped cream. We eat all kinds of stuff that is, well, a cheap imitation of what was once a really fine dish."

"Do you mean you know where the recipe is for my mother's Waldorf Salad, and I could make it and have it again?" Anne Henry asked. "Is it that simple?"

Mildred stood back up. "That's what I've been trying to say. That recipe Anne Henry wants is one that we just recalled together, and she can make it now. We can put that recipe in our cookbook as Anne Henry's mother's Supreme Waldorf Salad. Maybe Anne could write a memory of her mother and how her mother taught her something true about Jesus. Your mother did love Jesus, didn't she?"

"Absolutely," Anne Henry replied quickly. And then as if the question had a hint of criticism in it, she added emphatically, "And Jesus loved my mother."

"Even better," Fran added, standing back up and facing the roomful of women. "It could be a memorial cookbook to the women—and men—who left legacies of faith, and we would honor their memories with the recipes that we try to discover or concoct that come as close as they can be to a dish you may not have tasted in years but which you associate with them. We could help each other try to figure out the recipes just like we did right now with Anne Henry. We just need to tell each other the dish and describe it. One of us will know it or have a theory about it. That's a beginning."

"Twenty years," Mildred said, standing alongside Fran. "I've been trying to make my mother's sweet potato pie for twenty years, and I have never achieved it."

"What did it have in it?" I called out from the back.

"Sweet potatoes," Mildred replied.

"Don't you remember anything else?"

"I remember mama had her back to me while she was cooking, and I remember she used the can opener. My mother had a love affair with Vanilla extract, and I've added extra vanilla to various recipes for sweet potato pie that call for three and four eggs and dashes, pinches, or a half teaspoon of nutmeg and twice that of cinnamon and a cup or a whole can of evaporated milk. I've even tried heavy cream plus light corn syrup, but I cannot recreate my mother's signature sweet potato pie."

"Was the filling light like a custard?"

Mildred shook her head no.

"Was it heavy? Dense?"

"Yes," she replied, and something in her body shifted, and I thought: *'She's heavy with grief. She wants a piece of her mother's pie.'*

"I don't know if I'll ever be able to make that pie," Mildred confessed. "But what about all of you? Do you have dishes that you haven't made but you would like to eat and share with people you love but you don't have the recipe?"

Church lady heads all around the room nodded. There was a great taste for what had been, and it was more than nostalgia or a love for their mothers. It was an appetite for fellowship with the women and men who had helped set the tables for family life—family lives that had evolved through the years the way foods had. The recipes had changed, shifting here and there with lighter sugars and low-fat whipped creams and mayonnaise instead of heavy whipped cream and less of this and no fat at all until the pared down or swapped out ingredients resulted in a lesser version of old-fashioned dishes that had been rich in taste and tasted like an abundant love that was no more.

Lucy decided to call for a vote, and before she said the actual words all the ladies who had been standing as part of the discussion sat down. Lucy looked around the room and asked, "Do you want to pursue this idea—to investigate recipes and write stories about legacies of faith in our version of a cookbook?"

"It is a form of testifying," I said, from the back, surprising myself. My voice was too soft, so I said it again, more loudly. "It could be a form of testifying."

"I like remembering my mother," someone said, ignoring my comment. "My mother made stack cakes from dried apples. She dried apples on a tin roof. We don't have tin roofs anymore."

"We can find a way to dry the apples without a tin roof to do it on," Fran promised.

"Shall we try?" Lucy asked.

There was no need to vote. Heads nodded unanimously, even mine. For my own Uncle Johnny made a stuffed bell pepper that was his signature dish. He said he learned it while he was a chef for a grand hotel in California, but he really learned how to cook it in prison where he served time for stealing cars. I won't tell anyone that. And they won't tell me everything either. He got saved right before he died.

"What shall we call our cookbook?"

"Recipes from the Grave?" I suggested loudly.

Mildred turned around and leaned her arm on the chair, and I thought she was about to say something like 'That doesn't sound very appetizing,' but her face was serious. Mildred said, "I believe that title would attract attention."

So we called it that. And in it were the recipes for Fran's mother's banana bread made in a cast iron skillet and Anne Henry's mother's Supreme Waldorf Salad and Mildred's mother's sweet potato pie that no one believes is really the pie she pines for, but "it was close" she kept saying, like everybody else did because we all wanted to taste those dishes again so much. Trying to figure them out together was kind of fun; and at the last minute, someone asked the question—I don't remember who—if anyone knew what real banana pudding was supposed to taste like, and every woman in the room raised her hand. We have been eating knock-off banana pudding for most of our adult lives, and we are raising a whole generation of children who have never tasted real homemade banana pudding made from scratch. We had a big discussion about it—whether it would do anyone any real good to give people a taste of banana pudding glory and then expect them to eat the cold, gloppy mess that restaurants and churches serve for fellowship night, and I thought, 'No. No one but me is going to think we ought to put that recipe in the book,' but we did. I was surprised so many other people thought the same way I did, and I learned that while we made the cookbook. Knowing that made me feel less alone.

We also put a picture of Real Banana Pudding in all of its toasted meringue splendor on the front of the Circle's *Recipes from the Grave* cookbook. Every one of us pledged to make some real banana pudding in our own homes, and we cried some together about it because we all missed Real Banana Pudding and living with so many public lies told about it caused us to repent that we hadn't spoken up sooner. It was the only recipe we put in our cookbook that we were sure was right and true.

The other recipes were good, and we all tasted each other's memories of love that way. No one could really say that the dishes were perfect. We loved and honored our fathers and our mothers too much to say that.

We got closer though to tasting the love and the perfection of the past than we ever had before, and that's something.

9
PRACTICE BEING DEAD

"The average American spends about $35 every six weeks on haircuts," Mildred Budge announced suddenly to Fran Applewhite, picking up on a conversation about the work of missions at church that came and went all the time between them—ever since Mildred had been drafted to serve on the Go-or-Send missions committee. Everyone took a turn on that committee before they died, and no one had ever died while on the committee.

"So if we delayed getting our haircuts by one week and saved the price of one haircut and donated that annual savings of $35 to missions that would be quite a collection of missions dollars by the end of the year," Mildred Budge said, chewing momentarily on the tip of her left thumb in the way that she had once upon a time chewed upon a red pencil while grading papers.

Mildred Budge didn't grade papers anymore. Her red marking pencil had retired when she had. Mildred Budge was now a full-time church lady.

"Are we still talking about raising money for missions?" Fran asked unnecessarily. The question was a stalling technique while she gathered her wits.

"You know I'm still on the committee. They tried to kick me off last December, but I talked the missionsman into letting me stay on. I promised him that I was going to be a lot of fun on the committee from now on."

"You talked a man into something? I don't believe it, and I specifically do not believe that you used the word *fun* with the missionsman."

"It's true. The powers-that-be kind of asked the old-timers to leave the committee and make a space for someone younger; but I feel young at heart, so I argued that I simply wasn't finished yet."

"You're not finished yet?" Fran inquired delicately. The idea was loaded with danger and conceit. "You do know that anyone of us can die right this minute and life on the planet earth would go on just fine without us."

"I don't want to practice being dead today," Mildred replied immediately, emphatically. "I'm not finished. There's work to be done. The harvest is ripe, and the laborers are few. I want to have some fun."

Unperturbed, Fran replied, "I thought you were going to collect aluminum cans for recycling or have a garage sale or a bake sale for missions."

"The church doesn't like to sell stuff. It confuses people about the church being a marketplace, and Jesus doesn't like the church being used or seen as a marketplace. Do you remember how Jesus got out his whip?"

"Tell that to the politicians who use the name of Christ all the time to endorse themselves and raise money on TV," Fran said. She always said that when the discussion of selling stuff at church occurred.

Mildred nodded that she had heard her friend and then continued explaining her own agenda. "If I didn't have such a hearty respect for the church's position on that particular subject I'd have launched my missions calendar last year. We could put the big party dates on it, like the annual Mission's Conference, the Fall Bible Conference, the bar-be-que church-wide lunches, and the work days at the church to clean up the children's playground, the side lawn, and the parking lot. The calendar would be useful, and we could charge, maybe, ten dollars or so for it."

"You would still have to sell a church calendar at church, and the church doesn't like to sell stuff." Neither one of them said a word about the new cookbook *Recipes from the Grave* that had been quietly dispersed by word of mouth through the Circle meetings, and the money collected and deposited in the collection plate with the words, "For the children."

The church had not served knock-off banana pudding at a fellowship supper since it was released. It had been a quiet and profound triumph. Whenever anyone bought a copy of the cookbook from Kathy over at the bookstore, she left clutching it to her bosom, which said more about the contents of the cookbook than any other kind of book review so coveted by authors who made their living writing books.

Mildred grew pensive. "We could put out a stack of calendars where we distribute the church directories and say,

'Take one, but make a donation to missions—a kind of thank-you-for-the-calendar donation,'" Mildred suggested tentatively.

"Sounds like a lot of trouble to me," Fran said. "Promise me that you are not telling the missionsman all of these ideas of yours. Are you?" Fran asked delicately. "You know, men don't like a lot of words said to them very often. Even Dr. Phil says that."

"Dr. Phil talks more than anyone else on his television show and that includes the women guests that he routinely teases not to use too many words at home. Sometimes Dr. Phil is a little too pleased with himself."

"There's a name for that."

"And if Dr. Phil practiced being dead from time to time he might get over it."

"But back to the missionsman. You haven't been driving the missionsman crazy with these, well, ideas of yours, have you? Cause if you are he's not having much fun, and you promised him that you would be more fun than you usually are."

"I didn't tell him about the calendar idea, but I explained the haircut idea to him fully. Right when I was getting to the good part his cell phone buzzed in his pants pocket again, and he said, 'Gotta go.' So he had to go. He's very popular."

"Gotta go," Fran repeated, and she could almost hear the missionsman say those words in just the way that Mildred repeated them to her, only Mildred said them with shining eyes and a happy-hearted expectation that the missionsman understood and respected her plan to sacrifice vanity by postponing a beauty treatment to save the thirty-five dollars a year more for missions. Mildred's fundraising idea was chockful of Christian virtue if you looked hard enough.

Fran softened, and reached out a hand and patted her friend on the forearm where an age spot was beginning. It was hard to stay unspotted from the world when the sunshine made little brown dots on one's person. "Growing your hair out an extra week to save money and give it to missions is a sweet idea, Mildred. A very sweet idea."

"Do you really think so?" Mildred smiled broadly, her brown eyes shining like a kid's at the playground. Her lips needed color.

Fran looked closer, and she saw that the skin around her friend's eyes and nose was cracking from lack of moisture. Mildred forgot to tend to her skin and was often in need of a bottle of lotion or hand cream or eye cream or face cream. Fran resolved in that moment to put together a Mercy package for Mildred—the kind that the girls in the Berean class kept in the Sunday School room cabinet for one of them to grab and take with her to any gal-pal who got stuck in the hospital, where the artificial air dried you out, parching the Southern woman charm right out of you. The Berean-inspired, pre-packed gallon-size Ziploc bag called a Mercy gift package contained small bottles of hand sanitizer, shampoo, conditioner, lotion, face cream, toothpaste, little packets of instant decaf coffee, artificial sweetener, a small plastic comb, a packet of Kleenex, and a copy of Leah Slawson's truth-drenched devotional book *New Every Morning*. It was good company when you were feeling alone or afraid in the hospital.

Fran nodded, running her fingers through the back of her hair where her curls were sprayed to roll upwards, which brought a lift to her face, upon which gravity had taken a disappointing toll. She was still very pretty, and in a way, prettier than she had ever been in her long life though she did not know it.

"Let's cut to the chase. Let's apply the Golden Rule of Missions to it. Here's how it could sound summed up for the congregation: You just want people to donate the price of a haircut once a year by waiting a week longer throughout the year to get their hair cut."

"It wouldn't hurt people to wait an extra week throughout the year to get their hair cut. People don't look that good anyway. We spend a lot of money on tending to ourselves, and none of us looks that great."

"You didn't say that about people not looking too good to the missionsman, did you?" Fran asked.

"Yes. I had just finished saying that when his cell phone buzzed in his pocket, and he had to take the call."

"We need to let your idea simmer a while. It's never a bad idea to apply the Practice Being Dead rule as well as the Golden Rule of Missions to one of your ideas. Dr. Phil is right about men and words. Let them be few. Let them be really, really few. The fewer the better."

Mildred puzzled over the advice, and then wondered how much they could make on a church calendar given that shipping drove the cost per calendar up considerably and how soon would they need to have it put together and sent to the printer to get it ready in time for the new year. She continued to count and plan while she nodded silently to Fran, not saying a word, not even a few but not dead yet—not by a long shot.

Daphne Simpkins

10
IN YOUR EASTER
BONNET

Announcements for the Easter season began infiltrating the church newsletter just after Christmas. Whispered questions and answers about how Easter would be spent were shared in the hallways between Sunday School and the worship service.

"Are you going to the sunrise service?"

"Maybe. Kinda early for me."

In addition to the new Easter sunrise service there was going to be a special meal served on fellowship supper night and a guest speaker talking about the hope of heaven. In that way the emphasis on heaven was a surprise the way the Winter's Grace service had been at Christmastime. The recently introduced Winter's Grace service was offered to the people who had known great loss at Christmas and so had to muddle through all that jolly frivolity in a Christmas spirit not conducive to singing or laughing. They were faking it until they made it through the holidays.

Mildred Budge had attended the Christmas Winter Grace service and felt that it had been a wonderful time-out experience from noise, and she always welcomed silence. Silence created her preferred environment.

Easter seemed to lend itself naturally to a quiet experience of a profound hope. The message of the Resurrection pulsed up in Mildred frequently and not at her own bidding. Brief moments of knowing the hope of heaven had begun so long ago that she had lost track of any beginning.

Most vividly, there was the time when her friend Hugh had died suddenly and Mildred had been reaching for something in the cabinet and she knew, knew without any proof except for the way that time stopped inside of her and she too was transported instantly to an experience of paradise—just an instant, that's all it took—where her friend Hugh lived now. Really lived. In the knowing she was there for an Easter moment, and that one single moment in time spent with Hugh in paradise was always with her after that—part of many days and every Easter.

And there was that time when she was sitting on the pew in church, and she felt surrounded by a cloud of unseen angels, and she heard a kind of singing so close she couldn't not hear it and so far she couldn't make out the words. "Easter," she breathed.

And there was the unforgetting of Becky who had been her sister at church, and together they had planned the Easter egg hunts because children like to hunt for treasure and run around in the sunshine. Each year for about a dozen years, Becky had always gotten the plastic eggs and candy ready, and Mildred had always cleaned up her house and offered her big freshly mowed back field of a yard for the hunting grounds. At the end of every egg hunt Becky had always said, 'Same time next year, Millie?" And Mildred had always nodded and said, "Sure, Becky. Same time next year," except that last time.

During the last Easter egg hunt, Becky had stayed inside the borders created by the brim of that yellow calico Easter bonnet made by her grands to keep her bald head from getting sunburned on what would be her last outing. While she was outside with her friends after the last chemo session and was tuckered, Becky's gaze shifted slowly, absorbing the sights and sounds. Children were running underneath the softly rolling clouds. In previous years Becky had always stooped to pick up broken plastic eggs and bits of paper, not wanting to leave behind a mess for her friend Mildred, whom she had promised a dozen years before when they became co-hostesses of the annual hunt: "You provide the place, and I'll do the work." That last egg hunt, Mildred had provided the place, but Becky couldn't do her promised share of the work. So Mildred didn't see the scraps of candy paper and half shells of broken plastic Easter eggs either—not while her friend was nearby. When you are a friend to someone passing on into paradise soon you don't lean over to pick up trash when your old friend, who always prided herself on doing her share of the work by picking up the children's trash, could not even afford to notice it.

"We had another good time together," Becky said, coming slowly to stand beside her old friend Mildred Budge. But even that movement was a calculation—a strategic move to buy herself some time to get her breath. Mildred stood quietly, controlling the intake and release of her own breath so that she would not appear too strong, too healthy beside her dying friend. Mildred slowed her own breath to keep her friend's shallow breathing company. And there Mildred stood until Becky got her breath, and then with a slight wordless nod, tipping her calico bonnet like a farewell wave toward Mildred, Becky walked wordlessly away toward the car where another church-lady friend was waiting to drive Becky home from the last egg hunt she would attend.

As Becky gripped the door handle, every farewell for the past dozen years that happened every spring between Mildred and herself flashed right before her eyes. Mildred's, too. Becky knew the words Millie had always heard because she had always said them. Becky couldn't say farewell the same old way that day, however. Instead, after catching her breath, Becky waited until Millie looked right at her. Then Becky promised her old best friend, "I'll be seeing you later, Millie," and Mildred had nodded and not needed to blink back tears because those tears were so deep inside of her that it would take years for the grief to make its way to her eyes.

But over time and as more friends passed on into glory, the tears came all right. As time went by through the years when the sky was blue and the white clouds were rolling overhead and the next generation of children continued to run underneath them, Mildred often let herself weep at Easter over losing her friend. Easter after Easter she always thought of Becky in her butter-yellow calico Easter bonnet and her slow turning to go home, and after the tears and in spite of what else was going on at church or who the guest speaker was Millie Budge always said the same words before the Easter sun set one more time, "I'll be seeing you, Becky."

11

THE UNFAITHFUL WIDOW

"The big problem for me right now as a widow is that for the past forty-three years I was focused on him. Now, I look around and around and around, but he isn't here."

'Turn your eyes upon Jesus,' Mildred thought immediately; but even she, an unmarried woman, knew that a cliché was a wrong response when the friend in front of her who had just lost a part of her life more serious than a limb was telling her a singular and distinct truth: she was deeply disoriented. Her husband had died. He had been her focus. She didn't know where to look now.

Mildred waited, listening for that interior voice of counsel that Christians accept and, over time, learn to trust and obey and call by a variety of titles but not spouse. A spouse was a mystery to Mildred, as was the kind of loss that her friend was describing, but the Holy Spirit was alive and known and her Dear Companion. Guidance murmured inside of Mildred

Budge like a brook that flows unceasingly. Disciplined in listening to all of her friends, Mildred's attention split: the Brook murmured, *be still*, while her friend, the widow, continued to talk.

"I can't make sense of my life. He was here. He was always here. Then, he wasn't here. People came--lots of them. People left. The house was full. The house is empty. I wake up and remember he is gone, and then all day long as I plan the day, what to cook, what to iron, where to go, what to buy, I keep thinking what would he like, what would he want, what does he need, and he's not here, and so I have to think about what I want, what I might like, what I need. It isn't...." She almost said *natural*, but that wasn't the word she was searching for. The new widow struggled to explain and shook her head, bewildered by her condition.

As her friend struggled to locate the right word, Mildred imagined what the truth could be. She was not expecting the words her friend finally confessed.

"My life doesn't feel like home anymore. That's it. I am still here with all of this around me, but I am homeless."

"Home is where your heart is," Mildred said, ignoring her own advice not to speak in clichés.

"Exactly," her friend confirmed emphatically. "He died and took my heart and home with him."

"It's that bad," Mildred concluded softly, and there was awe in her voice, for home was the most powerful draw of any lifetime. More than food, drink, and physical intimacy, home stood for all of those things, and security, too. And the future—the future.

"It is that bad," her friend said.

Mildred sighed deeply, for she was out of wisdom and words, too. Widowhood needed a different set of vocabulary words.   The ordinary language of everyday pain wasn't enough to tell the truth of the human heart that feels homeless.

"I simply don't know what to do. I wake up every day, and I don't know what to do. Where to look."

The widow looked at Mildred finally, expecting wisdom.

Mildred felt silenced, dulled by all of the usual appropriate responses to human suffering: *In all circumstances give thanks; when God closes a door, he opens a window* (which was not in the Bible); *there are seasons for death and life.* But the only sound advice that emerged within her was not appropriate for her friend. It fit Mildred only: *It is better to go to a house of mourning than to a house of feasting.* She couldn't tell a widow that.

"Want to know something funny? I hate being hungry now. All those casseroles in my freezer, and I hate being hungry. It feels disloyal to be hungry when he isn't here to share my supper. I hate wanting anything now, too; it feels as if I am being disloyal to him. I hate making any kind of plan and doing it, because it feels like I am being unfaithful. We did things together. That's how it was. That's how it was supposed to be. I feel unfaithful being still alive, and I was always faithful. Always," she declared emphatically. "I loved him, Mildred. I still love him."

Mildred nodded, silently.

"I tried to go to a movie the other day and got as far as the ticket booth, and then I thought, 'I can't go in there without

79

him.' I can't go to a movie without him. We go everywhere together. Everywhere. And he left me.

"At church, I hate sitting on the same pew where we always sat because he's not going to join me now. His space stays empty. He used to give out the church bulletin and take up the collection, and then he joined me. He doesn't join me now, but I still feel as if I am waiting for him. He's not here. He's not coming back, and I am waiting for him. He left me, Mildred. I would never leave him, Mildred—never."

There was a terrible pause--a dreadful moment of silence when Mildred thought again that her friend expected her to say something, but Mildred had nothing to say. Nothing. It was an aching, terrible silence. Mildred was lost inside the terrible silence with her friend, and it was so great a silence that even the tears that should have sprung to her eyes in sympathy were too deep inside of her to reach the surface. There was a terrible vacancy where her friend's husband had been, and this terrible silence marked that place.

"Most of the time I am just trying to get through the day. A lot of people have given me advice. I've tried some of it. The boldest prayer I have tried is the 'make me content prayer' that I learned from Betty Little, but it only helped a little bit—like one Tylenol does against a migraine."

Mildred thought a Tylenol sounded good. She wondered if her friend would think her unfeeling, unfaithful, if she rummaged around in her purse for her portable pill bottle. She did feel as if she needed something for the pain that her friend was enduring and which she was now sharing. Mildred sighed deeply--groaned.

"But then I decided I wouldn't ask God for anything. Nothing. Not even contentment, because all of it—anything you could want-- all of it, felt unfaithful to my husband to ask. That's the only word that comes close to describing living like this without him. I feel like an unfaithful widow because I am still here."

Mildred's hand reached for her purse. She unzipped it-- plunged her right hand into it. Her fingers searched for the Tylenol bottle. Her friend might not take one, but she really needed something for the pain of this loss. Just sitting beside the pain of widowhood was hard.

But before Mildred could locate the bottle, her friend said, "The only thing that has helped—absolutely the only thing— is the 'God is sovereign prayer.' He gives and He takes. Blessed be the name of the Lord."

"Blessed be the name of the Lord," Mildred repeated automatically. Her pain receded slightly.

"That is the only thing that helps."

Mildred's hand let go of the pill bottle. She withdrew her hand from the purse.

"And so I pray that now pretty much all day long. The Lord giveth and the Lord taketh away. Blessed be the name of the Lord."

She inhaled, then said, "Do you want something to drink? We could have something to drink. I sure have been talking a lot, and I am thirsty. It was good of you to come, Millie. And thanks for not giving me any advice. There is no advice. There is only 'Blessed be the name of the Lord.'"

And as she said the words, the fresh widow finally, her heart broken, smiled.

12
SEE YOU IN HEAVEN

The older woman with short-cropped grey hair, a white blouse, and too-big-for-her blue jeans surveyed with delight the line of people waiting to buy stamps or mail a package at the post office. Her roving bright green gaze fell upon Mildred Budge, who nodded companionably and did not look away. It was part of Mildred's Christian calling in life not to avoid the animated gaze of others who needed a friend, but this woman did not exactly fit that category. She was the other kind: a woman who saw everyone in the whole world as her friend. Collecting her various items that she had been sorting at the table, the smiling woman joined Mildred Budge at the end of the long line of customers in the post office.

Her voice was musical, the syllables moving up and down as if she had spent time in India and learned their cadence as she asked of everyone in the line: "Isn't it a beautiful day?"

The line of waiting customers turned away, but not Mildred Budge, who earnestly believed that older ladies who spoke out loud in an incessant happy way in public should be responded to not only politely but with equal measures of joy asserted.

"Yes, indeed! After that storm we had last night, it is surprising to have such a beautiful day," Mildred replied.

"All those lightning strikes are good for the garden," the lady affirmed, brightly, her eyes rotating up and down the line in case someone else wanted to participate in the conversation between Mildred Budge and herself.

No one did. They kept their backs assiduously turned, focused on the task of mailing boxes, bills, and income tax statements. Mildred fought the urge to read the names and addresses on other people's envelopes. She knew the inclination was nosy and rude, but other people's lives always seemed so very interesting.

"I just need two stamps. I had stamps, but I left them at home. And now I must buy two stamps in order to mail my letters." She seemed quite happy about it.

"You are happy everywhere you go," Mildred stated, with a smile. She was often happy, too, but had learned to sublimate it so that she wouldn't look too foolish in public. Mildred resolved in that moment to look more undignified in the future, for it is the fear of being seen as undignified that keeps people so frozen in their places and often in their pews.

"Yes. I am still learning that the happiness I have is a kind of grace. I have been happy my whole life."

"I have too," Mildred confessed. "And I have a reason to be happy. His name is Jesus," she said.

"Oh, yes. We must always be willing to give a reason for the hope that we have in us. His name is Jesus," she agreed. Her grin grew wider. Her shining green eyes looked charged with electricity as if from the lightning strikes, and Mildred suddenly thought, 'She's like a garden, she is.'

"I told my sweet Jesus this morning that I was so grateful to pay taxes—to have so many jobs and have so many reasons to pay taxes," the other woman said, eyes gleaming. "Isn't it a great privilege to be able to work and support our government with our taxes? Our beautiful country!"

"I thanked our blessed Savior this morning for allowing me not to become rich and famous. It is my goal in life to die anonymously and almost poor," Mildred replied honestly.

"Put her there, Sister," the woman said, taking Mildred's hand and pumping.

"I have everything I need and a little more to share."

"A little more to share," Mildred murmured. "What a bounty that is."

"I just came from a celebration for a sister's fifty years of service. Think of that—fifty years of serving the Lord as a nun. It's inspiring."

"Forgive me, but you have something of a sisterly quality about you yourself," Mildred replied.

"I used to be a nun—a sister in that way too until I got my dispensation. I needed to leave my order because I just didn't have enough people to love there. I need lots and lots of people to love so I had to leave. Are you a nun?" She asked.

"Just a born-again Christian," Mildred said, wondering if it would be considered inappropriate to invite the former nun to come to her precious Sunday School class. This smiling woman would make a wonderful Berean class member, although she was considerably happier than most people Mildred went to church with or maybe there were many, many, happy, happy Christians who had steeled themselves to hide it lest they become a stumbling block for others.

"I know what kind of Christian you are," she said, patting Mildred's arm. "I can see right off that you know what matters. Jesus. The Time Keeper. The Threshold. The Gorgeous One. He's my Everything—my All in All. Yours, too."

"Mine, too," Mildred Budge agreed, simply.

They stared into each other's eyes to store the memory of the encounter, and the line moved up. Mildred bought stamps—what she needed and two extra to share, which she turned and gave to her newly met sister. They moved to the counter where they laughed out loud while they applied stamps to their respective envelopes. Then, each sister turned to place her envelopes into the specific mail slots their missives required; and as she walked out the door, her just-met sister called out loudly, her voice merry with joy and unrepressed hope, "Good-bye, Ladybug. See you in heaven if not before."

13

VOLUNTEERING WITH HOSPICE

A great and lonely shudder went through Fran Applewhite as she walked to her car from the office on Perry Hill Road, where she volunteered to help with the filing at the local hospice. She enjoyed going to an office where one still dressed up and where the aura of professionalism was present and understood, as common as the words *telephone* and *business hours.* Like other church ladies, she volunteered for a non-profit outreach ministry in the name of Jesus but also because she liked being out in the world though she was not of the world.

Fran's non-profit of choice was the local Baptist Hospice, where a bevy of beautiful ladies and handsome men befriended people who had life-ending illnesses but where it was always proclaimed honestly: "No one knows the last day of your life here except the Creator who gives it. We are here to keep you company and do what we can to make each day as good as it can be."

Fran Applewhite lived on those words, though daily, sometimes hourly, in the company of Mildred Budge or not, Fran often moaned a deep and shuddering prayer of "Take me anytime you want to, Jesus. I'm ready." But there was nothing in that moan that was despairing-- just honest and the very real reason that Fran had never in her whole life spilled the beans of her life story or the story of her moans to a preacher. Neither had her friend Mildred Budge, and neither one of them in the whole length of their glorious friendship had ever explained to the other one why she had not told the story of her life to a preacher or asked his counsel. There were great places of privacy that each woman respected in the other, and each woman respected the walk of the other with the One who always walked with you. His name is Jesus.

"It was a hard day, Jesus," Fran whispered over the steering wheel as she turned out of the parking lot and onto the main road that would take her back to her neighborhood, where her house would be dark and quiet, sitting in the shadows waiting for her.

As usual, a woman who subscribed to the benefits of self-discipline, Fran gave herself the length of the drive home—fifteen minutes or so—to sift through the events of the morning at the hospice office. Every phone call was a drama. Every person who helped other people was a person who needed help. All the people at hospice were strong people; and because they were very strong and dependable, they were often not prayed over as they might have been. Sometimes Fran thought that her whole mission at hospice was to pray for the very strong and dependable people who worked there and kept company with the dying and their family and friends who were grieving already.

The attending professionals—nurses and aides-- of the hospice came and went on regular calls and emergency calls. In between at the office they talked about their own lives and often made phone calls to their own families in the room where Fran did the filing, and where she, priestlike, heard but never appeared to hear and never ever discussed the content of what she heard with anyone, including Mildred Budge. The content of the early phone call by a hospice nurse to her husband that very morning was now stored in the inner part of herself where Fran kept the world's secrets as most church ladies learned to do, priestlike.

The nurse had been speaking to her husband on the phone, updating her to-do list for what should happen should she predecease her husband.

"If I die first make sure our daughter goes to college, and if I die first go ahead and get married again but wait until our daughter goes off to college because I don't want another woman living in my home making my daughter's life miserable. And give my jewelry to my baby. Don't you give my good jewelry to your next wife, whoever she turns out to be."

And after that, the determined nurse had fought the urge to slam down the phone but, through will and after twenty years as a hospice nurse, she carefully placed the phone down. Then she sat in silence and stillness while Fran had kept her back to her, filing, filing, hearing and keeping the secrets of a broken world in her heart. Fran Applewhite could file so silently that sometimes she was invisible.

At last the nurse had inhaled deeply and exhaled a confession: "I see you over there filing, Miss Fran. I know you heard me, Miss Fran. You hear everything. I know you don't talk, but I don't care who you tell. If I die first, you call up my husband and you tell that man o' mine what I said—you're a witness!-- and that he better do what I said, or else."

Fran stiffened at the request. Her hands kept filing.

There was no rebuttal to a woman's threat of "or else" from the grave. The nurse was in no imminent danger of expiring; but hospice nurses, like lawyers who drafted last wills and testaments, were forever getting their own houses in order should they make an unexpected departure from this world to the next. They were very practiced at being dead—had rehearsed what came after their own deaths more than anyone Fran knew. Fran thought of her own house. It was well maintained, and her furnishings were as pared down as could be with just enough stuff to have to dust more than she wanted to dust.

Fran let herself nod that she had heard the nurse and that she would fulfill that last request if necessary. But she said nothing out loud. Her hands kept filing.

The nurse had walked over and patted Fran on the back and said, forgiving her for being a silent witness, "See you later." Then she had left to help others feel better and answer the questions that most people should ask and answer more often than they did: "What do you want the day to be like today?

What quality of life are you seeking? Let me help you achieve that."

No cliché ever came out of people who were making a final exit soon. So often they replied with surprise in their eyes and wonder in their voices: "I want to eat a bowl of ice cream every night, and I want to watch a football game."

It was very comforting to discover that when death was imminent the ordinary routine of your ordinary life was the extraordinary last request of an ideal day.

Twenty years ago, when Fran had started volunteering for hospice, she had been surprised that all of the big dreams of people's lives had become that mundane, and there was no disappointment that they had scaled down their desires to these daily portions. There was a great relief in it.

And it had caused Fran to do the same—to measure her days according to the truth of her real confessed human ambitions instead of what the world told you that you should want and spend your time and energy and resources trying to gain. Fran wanted less and less of anything the world had to offer as time went by, and the surprise was that surrendering ambition and desire had created a void that had been filled by an immense love and an energizing lit-up joy that kept her company in a fresh and wondrous way.

These were the truths Fran lived on now, marveling time after time that so many wives said of their husbands while they were dying, "I had me a good one....my husband," and they had found satisfaction, fulfillment, causes to be grateful in a good one who had persevered and who was not rich and famous--only faithful and kind. No big money. No big glamour. A good one was an ordinary person, and the world didn't proclaim the virtues of living with someone who would also just like a bowl of ice cream and to watch the football game with you. Fran was telling herself and Jesus that story again as she drove home, sorting out the details only to be interrupted by the appearance of flashing blue lights in her rear view mirror. Fran checked her speed. It was fine.

Fran slowed her car as the patrol car raced around her. She saw then what the patrolman was headed toward: two cars had slammed hard into each other. An ambulance was coming, too, Fran saw, checking her mirror as more sirens blasted. She kept driving, her peripheral vision taking in the sight of a man standing befuddled by the open door of his damaged car and a driver from the other car lying in the grass with a pair of blue pajama bottoms displayed on one leg. The rest of him had been covered in a blanket. The hospice volunteer took note of his covered face and the lifeless bare leg and what his covered face meant. Automatically, with her very next breath, Fran Applewhite, Gritz's widow, Winston's fiancé, Mildred Budge's best friend, hospice volunteer, church lady of the South, identified herself completely by saying one word, one name that was everyone's story all the time and forever and the only hope of any plan about how to live and how to die. "Jesus," the church lady breathed, and kept driving as she did day after day, running her own kind of race toward home.

14
THE DOGHOUSE FELLOWSHIP

"So how it came to be was that an elder who kept asking me to serve on various committees would, before the time served on the committee reached its conclusion, get mad at me about having a different point of view than his, and he would put me in the Doghouse."

"What do you mean by Doghouse, exactly?"

Dixie asked Mildred Budge, who was trying to explain to Dixie, the newly converted church member, how people in a church were inclined to beat each other up in the name of Jesus in church and through the years had to find ways to stop doing that in church.

"Just as there was with Cain and Abel and Joseph and his brothers, there is a great deal of sibling rivalry inside the family life called church," Mildred said, taking the familiar position of fifth grade teacher with Dixie, who, she was afraid, might not have read enough of the Old Testament to recognize the siblings in question. However, Mildred thought that Dixie might have a better understanding of sibling rivalry than most people, for she suffered from multiple personality disorder.

Dixie's sibling-like personalities who lived inside of her continually jockeyed for dominance. Mildred talked most often with the woman who answered to the name Dixie, and who came to visit and talk about matters of the church and of the heart.

Dixie's response in the form of a question was reassuring. "Didn't Cain kill his brother Abel?" she asked.

"Oh, yes," Mildred said. "And Joseph's brothers sold him into slavery and told their dear father Jacob that his favorite son was dead, and they didn't stop telling that lie for years. It wasn't until a famine sent the whole kit and caboodle of them to Egypt for food that they found out that the brother they thought was dead...."

"Joseph?" Dixie clarified.

"Yes. Joseph was second in command in Egypt by then and in charge of doling out the food to starving people. Then his brothers—his original family-- were starving and needed him to give them food, and they were the ones who had tried to kill him."

"Ouch," Dixie said.

"Ouch, indeed. Anyway, sibling rivalry is as common in real life as it is in the Bible, and I haven't even mentioned the mother of the two brothers who were also apostles. She wanted her boys to sit on Jesus' right and left side, beating out the other apostle-brothers who might also have liked to sit closer to Jesus in his kingdom. I've always wondered if that was her idea or theirs. If so, did they put their mother up to it?"

"Bless her heart. She just didn't know what she was saying," Dixie replied.

"Bless her heart, indeed, and that's what Jesus said too," Mildred Budge agreed. "People find a way to compete with each other whether they're siblings or not. In church, people are at times moved by these kinds of impulses. In the running of the race, people still want to be the ones who get there first, and for a long, long time I kept serving on various committees with an elder who would get mad at me and put me in the Doghouse. He felt I impeded the successful completion of his God-ordained race by not consistently agreeing with him."

"Where is the Doghouse at church?" Dixie asked, sensibly.

The reasonable question asked about the Doghouse's physical location comforted Mildred about Dixie. A smile played at the corners of Mildred's mouth as she explained, "In the beginning the Doghouse existed in the elder's mind, but the experience of it got expressed as public rudeness. He stopped talking to me. If I asked a question his answer was dismissive. Sometimes he didn't answer me at all. "

"He gave you the silent treatment?" Dixie pressed. "And you called that the Doghouse?"

"From time to time, yes," Mildred said, smiling sunnily.

"And he did this often enough so that you came to expect a silent treatment in his appointed Doghouse when you said yes to his requests for your voluntary participation on different committees because you knew from past experience that eventually you would disagree with him and he would stop liking you for a while?"

Mildred nodded, thoughtfully.

"And you said yes anyway to working with him though you knew what would probably happen. Why would you do that?"

"There is a great deal of work to be done in just making a church operate. You can't get in a snit and refuse to do your share of the work just because you are likely to spend some time in the Doghouse before the work is completed. That experience of being in the Doghouse if you disagree with him just becomes part of the work. And there was always the hope that one of us would grow up enough to get over irritating the other one."

Dixie leaned forward and asked in a whisper. "You just honestly at times disliked each other?"

"Yes. That was hard to admit because you're supposed to smile sincerely at each other in church out of respect for that second commandment from Jesus that we love each other as ourselves."

"Love each other as ourselves..."

There was a dreadful pause while the implications of how that kind of neighborly love might feel to Mildred with her stolid, centered personality and how it might feel to Dixie, who was so very populated.

"Yes."

"Who is the elder who put you in the Doghouse?"

"Sam Deerborn."

"I know him. He's one of your best friends."

Mildred nodded.

"How did that happen? When did you two become the friends you are today?"

"Well, one day, Sam put me in the Doghouse after I voted no about a recommendation to spend some church funds on something I didn't think we needed to buy, and he got really exasperated with me and muttered under his breath—'Obstinate woman.'"

"You knew right then that you were headed to the Doghouse again?"

"I stopped in my tracks because history was repeating itself."

"Cain and Abel. Joseph's brothers. The two apostles. You and Sam?"

Mildred nodded. "So I finally said, in my obstinate way, 'Enough.' I stopped myself from leaving the room. I turned right around and said to Sam, 'If I'm going to the Doghouse, you're going with me.'"

"Did he know what you were talking about?"

"No. He had no idea that his actions were a form of public exile—like putting me in stocks or in time-out. It shocked him enough to listen to me. So I went right back over there and said, 'From now on when you start muttering under your breath and calling me names, we are both going to the Berean Sunday School classroom and sit in our respective hardback chairs for a whole hour and do absolutely nothing.'"

"What do you mean—do absolutely nothing?"

"I meant we weren't going to be reading our Bibles, weren't gonna be praying, couldn't be talking on the phone. We had to be quiet and absolutely fruitless. No fruit at all could be physically produced by us and our hands and mouths while we were in the Doghouse."

"Ouch. That is a terrible punishment for the two of you. You both like to work."

"Ouch, indeed. That got Sam's attention."

"How'd you make him go with you? It's not like he had to go, and from what I've seen in him and heard about him, he's kind of contrary."

"I pointed to the preacher who was standing nearby...."

"You said that in front of a preacher? Weren't you afraid that the preacher would think you are a trouble-maker? I'm very worried about that. I am afraid to talk in front of the preacher."

"Sure. But sometimes you just have to take a risk. The preacher seems fairly normal once you get to know him."

"I'm not sure I'm in a position to recognize what normal is. I'll take your word for it."

"Anyway, I said loudly enough for the preacher and anyone else standing by to hear: 'Sam and I are putting ourselves in time-out, where we both belong. I'm not saying we don't. And the preacher is going to come check on us in the Berean Sunday School classroom.' I looked hard at the preacher to make sure he heard my request."

"The preacher himself was going to be in charge of coming to check on you two in time-out?" Dixie clarified.

"I smiled at the preacher right then, and he couldn't help himself. He smiled back, and that really ticked off Sam because he thought I was getting the preacher on my side by smiling at him first. And maybe I was. We are all very sly in our own devilish ways."

"What I don't understand is why in the world would you want to be in the Doghouse with the man who likes to put you there?

"Oh. I've always loved Sam—some years more than others. There were just times when I couldn't stand him, and he couldn't stand me. There have been times when I deserved to be in the Doghouse at church, but because being with him so often caused those times I just didn't think it was right for me to have to be in the Doghouse by myself."

"If you say so," Dixie said skeptically.

"Sam started muttering immediately, and right then we adjourned to the Doghouse—that is, physically speaking, the Berean Sunday School classroom. There we sat in our time-out chairs. You should have seen Sam's leg. He couldn't keep it crossed. It was jumping up and down. He couldn't keep it still. And I was very composed. Very still."

"You were showing off a little bit, weren't you? Women are better at keeping still than men are. That's why men get to take up the money and serve communion. It's harder for them to sit still in the pews."

Mildred nodded, okay—that explanation would do for now. "I watched that poor old leg of his jumping up and down. And after a while I felt sorry for him and his leg, but I didn't say anything. And then he got a bad case of dry mouth. He was having trouble swallowing, and I saw he was thirsty. I had to fight the terrible urge to get him a glass of water in the name of Jesus. I wanted to help him; but by my own rule, I couldn't."

Dixie leaned forward. "Did you have to go to the bathroom?"

"Oh, yes. There's nothing like the idea of not being able to go to the bathroom that makes you need to go to the bathroom."

"How many minutes passed before you were just plain miserable?"

"About five minutes. Fifty-five minutes to go before the time-out was over."

"Oh, my. Hell."

"Sort of. And then something extraordinary happened."

"The angel Gabriel appeared with a message from God?" Dixie asked hopefully. She had extreme ideas about the Bible coming to life in front of her.

Mildred dismissed the idea readily. "Better than that. The preacher came in to check on us and saw us sitting there in such a terrible strain. He felt sorry for us and pulled up a chair and put himself in time-out with us."

"Oh my word. I have never heard of anything quite so shocking."

"Preacherman had heard the rules, and he obeyed them, smiling. I will always love that about him. He smiled at both of us but didn't say a word, and we all kept mum."

"A preacher kept mum?"

Mildred nodded. "And he has built his whole preaching career on the word *exposition*."

"It's kind of a miracle," Dixie marveled.

"There's more. It wasn't too long before the musicman walked by and saw the preacherman in there with two other people. Standing in the doorway, he waited for someone to speak to him; and when we didn't, he figured we were having a silent prayer time. Respectfully the musicman tip-toed in and sat down right next to me. He got awfully nervous about how quiet the room was though. He's accustomed to a lot of music, and at first, the silence made him nervous. He reached out and patted me on the knee in a kind of friendly greeting, like 'hello, there, how ya doing?' The preacher and Sam saw the musicman pat my knee, and then the musicman realized that he hadn't meant to pat my leg like that.   He got embarrassed and laughed out loud over how silly we all looked and how uncomfortable he was in silence. The sound of his laughter was so abrupt...."

"Oh, yes. I can just hear it. Like a horn blast that sounds behind you at the traffic light when you have stopped at a red light and the light has changed and you are holding up the other drivers and suddenly know it."

"Yes, sort of like that sound. But very soon, the musicman became silent too. He kind of drifted into a deep silence, and he closed his eyes. I think he hears music playing in his head all the time, and it looked like he really needed to be silent for a while. Everything in him went still. The preacherman saw it too—saw the musicman relax inside silence—and he held up one finger to his pursed lips and breathed softly, 'Sssh.' We were all so moved by musicman's sudden and deep relaxation into silence that we sat back in our chairs the way you do when you are a parent and a sickly child has finally fallen into a sleep that will help him get well. Then, we were watching the clock but not hard watching it—just paying it our respectful attention. Sam's leg settled down, and the warm spot on my knee that the musicman had created by touching me faded into nothingness the way anger does when you realize you are not really angry at anyone but yourself."

"Not really angry at anyone but yourself," Dixie repeated in wonder.

Mildred nodded, and she unconsciously patted a place on her knee that had once been very warm but wasn't any longer. "Anyway, other people who were in the church building sort of heard by word of mouth that we were in there being quiet together. One by one, they joined us—each one putting him or herself in time-out in the Doghouse with Sam, preacherman, the musicman, and me. The room filled up pretty fast. The moneyman sat in the corner next to the window and looked out, and I wondered what he was thinking about and where he would rather be. The missionsman showed up and joined us, and later I teased him that he had been able to go on a kind of mission trip in the Doghouse and never leave the building. He didn't think that was funny, but I always smile when I remember that excruciatingly exquisite time in the Doghouse with him.

"Then the minutes became as nothing, and the experience of time changed. It felt light and airy—eternal, sort of. And way down at the other end of the hallway someone in the kitchen figured we all had to be thirsty and made a pitcher of Kool-Aid usually reserved for the children's nursery. Sweet Lorna brought us a tray of cherry Kool-Aid with small kid-size paper cups and a package of store-bought cookies, like the kind they serve over at the Respite Center at the Methodist church. You buy them at the Dollar Store."

"Butter cookies with no icing," Dixie clarified. "We grew up eating those cookies. All of us."

"They are good for a crowd," Mildred said, smiling softly because Dixie was trusting her with the kind of inside information that she didn't share with everyone. "Yes. They snap good, and they taste pretty good with cherry Kool-Aid. And when our hour was up it seemed too short actually, but we each had a cup of that Kool-Aid and a cookie, and all around the room people looked refreshed, less tense. We were at ease—had forgotten and forgiven all the trespasses real or imagined-- and it was a great feeling."

"I'd like to feel like that right now. I bet a lot of people would like to hang out in the Doghouse with you. You could call it the Doghouse Ministry."

"We all talked about that later. Sam and I almost got mad at each other again trying to figure out how we could make it happen."

"He's such an old fusspot."

"Yes. He's adorable," Mildred agreed. "But we decided not to use the word ministry. That word can become troublesome. We just call it the Doghouse Fellowship. It's where the sinners go to repent. Cool off."

"I like Doghouse Fellowship better," Dixie approved.

"You get over yourself, remember that you love other people as yourself, and find out that sometimes when you don't love others it is actually yourself you don't love. Time passes, and then you have what they serve children in the nursery: Kool-Aid and Dollar Store cookies."

"I want to go the next time you have it. Can we come?"

"Sure. Someone's always getting riled up about something at church; and when that happens, someone who remembers the benefits of a time-out jabs a thumb toward the Berean Sunday School classroom, and they go right there to a cool-down by doing nothing. It happens periodically throughout the year, but so spontaneously it never shows up formally on the church calendar. When it happens though news travels pretty fast, and a lot of people show up. Everyone is welcome at the Doghouse Fellowship."

"Or they could just come to church on Sunday mornings."

Mildred grinned. "Yes. If they miss the Doghouse Fellowship, they can just come to church on Sunday mornings."

15
DIXIE ATTENDS A MISSIONS MEETIN'

"They were some of the most bare-boned, plain-vanilla prayers I have ever heard, and that's the truth," Dixie said, after being allowed to sit in on a planning committee for the Missions Conference. It was a one-of-a-kind meeting, where church members who weren't officially serving on the conference planning committee were invited to sit in--to watch and listen and find out for themselves what went on literally behind the scenes before the big annual event. Dixie was a new church member, and she had been invited to attend the meeting for politeness' sake and because people liked Mildred Budge and Dixie was Mildred's friend—friends, actually. The new convert had multiple personality disorder and had as many mood swings as ten women going through menopause together.

People knew how to say the words that described Dixie's condition, but they didn't really know what it all meant any more than they understood everything about themselves and all the selves they had been and left behind through the years as the Holy Spirit sent by the Risen Savior led them through the cleaning process, expertly winnowing out various aspects of their human natures--events of change that were pointed to with words like repentance, confession, and new life and hope.

Dixie's own population of personalities seemed like a real big problem to others when they first heard about it, but they quickly relinquished any impulse to try and solve it, trusting that the formidable retired school teacher Mildred Budge could handle the unruly bunch of people casually referred to as Dixie.

After the first hushed whispered curiosity occurred questioning what might have caused Dixie's broken condition, interest faded quickly. Curiosity about Dixie passed into the past as it had about Mildred Budge, too.

This fading interest in each other at church was so normal no one paid much attention to it. This shift from being seen by some and becoming invisible to more and more people at church happened for a number of reasons that no one really named out loud, but the condition existed in the way that people instantly assessed one another by power, appearance, money, influence, marital status, widowhood, and sometimes authority at church.

Retired school teacher Mildred Budge looked different than she had when actively employed, rising every day at 4 am to pray for her students and then off to work at 7 am. The expressions on her face changed too after retirement. Sometimes she didn't even look like herself anymore.

Letting go of her responsibilities in the classroom had changed Miss Budge's face, which had become more vulnerable and open. She looked like other people who had retired or become widowed.

"What else happened last night in the planning meeting?" Mildred asked, while assembling the ingredients for a trial-run wedding cake. She was trying to perfect a wedding cake recipe for widows who were getting married a second time. She had an idea in mind of how the ideal cake should taste and look, but she hadn't succeeded in her quest to invent the perfect Encore Wedding Cake.

"A man read the Bible to us. I liked him very much though the people around the table wore funny looking faces while he read the Bible because I think he read it longer than they wanted him to. It's funny how people measure time. Everyone is supposed to love the Bible, but you're not supposed to read it aloud for too long in a meeting because the people who are supposed to love the Bible get tired of listening if the reading takes up so much time that they are late getting home to supper."

"The meeting is only supposed to run an hour," Mildred said quietly, for she knew that man, and he did have a love affair with the Bible. Further he had been retired a while, and no one listened to him talk much anymore. When he read the Bible aloud people had to listen to him.

Dixie sighed, her personalities resting in the background. "I was surprised that they didn't pray more. Everyone talks to each other more than they talk to God in front of each other, and I guess they go home and pray the rest of what needs to be said."

Mildred's face broke into a broad smile as she peeled the paper from a third stick of butter. The previous cake effort had been too dry, and she was trying to moisten this batter with more butter. She pushed the bowl with three sticks of butter aside to soften to room temperature and asked, "What else is there to say to God, Dixie?"

"Lots and lots. Everything all day long and all night. He's the only One who listens to me the way you listen to me. It helps being alive to be heard."

Mildred would have asked Dixie what she said to God, but she didn't have to know the details. No matter their differences, men and women shared many conditions in common: heartbreak and loneliness and despair and fortitude and isolation and hope and faith and misgivings and uncertainty and surprise and questions, like 'What if it's not real?' and 'What if I have talked myself into believing this because it is easier than facing life any other way?'

"There were a lot of angels in the meetin' room," Dixie announced suddenly. "They were all over the place, but the people sitting at the table didn't seem to know that."

Mildred had just cracked a fifth egg to separate the yolk from the white in order to achieve a texture and color she had in mind for both the cake and meringue-based white cloud frosting when Dixie announced that revelation.

'What to do?' There was the egg yolk tipping precariously from the shell, and there was the bowl of egg whites. The perfect recipe for a perfect wedding cake was waiting to be discovered; yet, Mildred Budge tossed the broken egg into the sink and gave her full attention to Dixie.

"Angels get lonely too," Dixie announced. "But they would. They are tending to people who won't talk to them and can't hear them, but their job is to tend to people."

The sun filled up the room, flooding Mildred Budge and Dixie and pulsed everywhere—alive, alive, and alive.

"Lots of angels in the room?" Mildred Budge asked. She couldn't help herself.

"Oh, yes. The room was full of them, and there were some more angels outside the room too. The missionsman's angels marched most of the time. There were six of them, and I could hear them outside marching back and forth up and down the hallway." Dixie's expression changed, and her face lit up animatedly. "You can hear a lot of history in the footsteps of angels. You could hear a steady walk at first but the further down the hall they went, the faster they walked and then at the end of their sentry run they turned in a hurry and double-stepped back as if they were afraid something would happen to their boy while they were at the end of the hall. You could hear the rhythm of troops from all over the world and times' past in the angels' footsteps—like drum sounds in a way. But these angels have always kept the military men company, and they are the missionsman's angels now. But he didn't hear them."

"He didn't hear them," Mildred repeated dully. She didn't know what else to say.

"There was a funny angel in the back of the room who was kind of muscle-bound, and when you saw him it was like he didn't know exactly what to do with his body. He is like us in that way," Dixie mused. "It is like he stepped off of a painting by Picasso for there was a blue light about him, and his features seemed geometrical—mostly planes and squares."

"He didn't know what to do with his angel body?" Mildred pressed.

Dixie nodded matter of factly as if what she had said was completely normal to say out loud.

"He had very big muscles in his arms and his chest was big—broad—and he wore a white t-shirt that was a size too small." Dixie closed her eyes remembering, and then as if she were providing an eye witness report to some official, she added, "There was writing on his chest with an important message for mankind. He has always worn that message. Always!" Dixie said, slapping the kitchen table suddenly. The bowl of butter bounced once and the two bowls with separated eggs and whites jiggled.

Instinctively Mildred reached out to the bowls and touched each one, reassuring herself that the ingredients for her wedding cake would be all right until she could get back to them.

"What did the message say?" Mildred asked. She couldn't help herself.

"You had to lean forward and concentrate to see the message because the words were in a foreign language and they were swimmy—like music notes. It wasn't just words, and it wasn't our alphabet either. I guess you could call them symbols, but if you looked close enough and squinted you kind of knew what they meant. I think that message on his chest was a law of physics that Einstein didn't live long enough to discover for himself. A lot of people know it, but Einstein never learned it. The words on his chest made a melody for us. I can still feel that melody—that message-- simmering here," Dixie said, pressing her hand to the center of her chest. "It hums all the time inside of me now. I find it very comforting—not like, well, other sounds inside yourself."

"Were there any words like ours at all?"

"You can't say those words on his chest. You can only hum them."

Dixie smiled and settled back in her chair. "I didn't know the tune, but I hummed it later for the rest of the night until I learned it. It is a kind of prayer." Dixie let her breath course through her and a faint melody hid itself in her humming. She seemed undisturbed that what she was humming had no strong melody to boast of, and it didn't have words to go with it. But the meaning mysteriously and authoritatively pulsed portentously from the sound of the music all the same.

"It was unceasing worship, wasn't it?" Mildred asked solemnly. The three sticks of butter in the bowl continued to soften, the egg whites became a small lake of composed motion, the golden egg yolks floated inside their confinement, and the three cups of sifted white flour sitting in its own bowl far, far away on the counter looked suddenly like a snow drift.

"If you say so," Dixie replied simply. "The preacher's angels were the busiest. They came and went. They had a hard time settling down. They were restless but vigilant. They kept checking on preacherman and the rest of us. In all kinds of ways we are part of preacherman though we don't feel like that because he stands so far away; but we are all together in a way. His angels look after him and keep an eye on all of us too—for him, I guess. They dart here and there; but they like to hang out down by the Alabama River. That is where they wait for the preacher to join them, but he never does. He's too busy."

"How do you know they were down by the river?"

"I could see them from where I was." Dixie's brow furrowed. "We can see more than we want to really know if we aren't afraid to look," she confessed, and then appeared startled by what she said.

"Do you know what the angels were doing down by the river?" Mildred asked. She couldn't help herself.

"Oh, yes. They were burying their feet in the mud by the water, and they wanted the preacher and us to come and do the same thing."

"Play in the mud?"

"It would be very good for him and us too, don't you think?"

Mildred considered that question and felt the oddest desire to hurry over to the Alabama River and take off her shoes and press her bare feet deep into the cool mud that runs alongside the shore of the river. And in the idea she could almost feel it—the contact with the dirt, the mud, the seeping and flowing water, blades of grass here and there-- the earth, this Eden. Water and earth. Oh, how Mildred had lost touch with the earth itself as she had grown up and become so dignified always wearing shoes everywhere she went. Mildred instinctively wiggled her toes inside her shoes, and suppressed a giggle that got born in her. The old school teacher hadn't giggled in so long that she thought she was about to get the hiccups before she realized it was, well, it was just a giggle.

Dixie smiled, turning her head as she looked around the room.

'Seeing what?' Mildred wondered.

"I see angels sometimes, but that's normal for me." Dixie turned toward Mildred, and her face became a sunflower— innocent and hopeful. "Do you believe me?"

It was an important question to ask—an important question to answer. So much of faith expressed depended upon someone taking the risk to share the interiority of a kind of life that is beyond the physical and attempts to share that faith using puny, puny words organized by struggling, inept, pride-damaged reasoning skills. The truth of human experience was broad and included hoping in the Divine, imagining Love, hungering and thirsting after truth and righteousness, and forgetting how to giggle.

Retired school teacher Mildred Budge who had kept company with children through the years and made friends with their friends—all kinds of friends, imaginary or otherwise—let her teacher's face smile and replied sincerely, "I believe you."

Dixie's shoulders relaxed. They had been held in tension until that moment, but in Mildred's acceptance of her and the respect the school teacher paid Dixie for the risk she was taking in telling the truth using puny, puny words, a kind of self-protection that most people wore throughout their life was laid down. Dixie felt safe, and it changed her. "I like angels, but I feel sorry for them but not as sorry for them as I do a couple of those people on the committee. They looked so worn down—defeated-- in their work, though there was a flicker of something last night when the man who read the Bible so long told everybody afterwards that they had a duty and a responsibility to support the work of missions. People perked up for a minute or so, and all the angels saluted him. Their salutes happened lickety-split, faster than a speeding bullet and were altogether. Really fast. They do it a lot. Every time someone pays his respects to the mission of the Man, they salute just like this." Dixie emulated the salute of the angels, and Mildred was surprised by how fast Dixie's hand rose to her brow, tipped against her temple, and returned to her side as if no salute had occurred at all, but it had. A faint breeze happened which proved it.

"Duty and responsibility, yes," Mildred said. She knew the words very well, and had given up the impulse to salute years ago. She couldn't remember when. It was difficult to know exactly when someone learned to keep their hands so still at their sides when there were so many words that made you want to raise your hand in a salute or both hands in prayer.

"All around the room the angels of everybody were at full attention and stood silently against the walls. One of the angels was very tall, almost seven feet tall. Modigliani caught a glimpse of him once and infused some of his portraits with that long, willowy look. Yes, tall, long. Willowy. Well, this willow tree of an angel kissed his long, long fingertips and placed the very tips of his exquisitely pale fingertips on the head of the woman across from me who had an awful headache. She kept holding her face in her hands she hurt so bad, and every time she drooped, her angel transferred a kiss from his humming lips to his tingling fingertips and then pressed the consolation of his kiss onto her head like this," Dixie said. Using three fingers only, Dixie kissed her own stubby fingertips and then pressed them onto the top of Mildred Budge's head.

It was the loveliest sensation in the world.

"Right after the angel kissed her, the woman would look up as if she knew something had happened; but the pain got to her pretty fast, and her head would dip again. The angel never stopped though. As soon as the pain slammed into her and she drooped, he would deliver a heavenly kiss again, but the relief never lasted. Why do you suppose the relief from an angel's kiss doesn't last very long?"

"Beauty is temporary and eternal," Mildred replied without hesitation. Paradoxes exist.

"There was only one time when all the angels began to hum at the same time, but no one else seemed to hear them. It was a pretty sound, as far as humming goes. I got the feeling that if they ever cut loose they would be able to sing extremely well. Extremely well!" Dixie said, and her voice changed. Suddenly the Dixie who had been reporting became another Dixie, and the veil that lifted to reveal this other girl happened so swiftly that Mildred had to stop and marvel that the experience of time and the coming and going of humanness in its variant forms and moods was transient and unexpectedly extreme.

'What relationship did human mood have to do with the eternality of beauty, if any?' Mildred wondered, but she knew that the question was as off point as the one about what had happened to Dixie to cause her to have so many personalities in her. What was the origin of Dixie's fragmented personality? If she were to become whole in the way that most people considered being whole, would she still be able to see angels? Who would ever want to give up seeing angels and hearing them hum just to be considered normal by the rest of a broken world?

Mildred thought she might ask Dixie if she saw any angels in the room with the two of them right then, but it seemed inappropriate to invade the privacy of the angels. The story of history was one thing; the seeing of angels in the here and now in this present light was another situation altogether. Mildred had a delicate sensibility about angels. If they wanted her to know they were nearby, they would let her know themselves. If someone else could see them, well, that was the other woman's blessing and the angels' business. Mildred did wonder about the music of them, however, for there were times when she was aware that there were angels singing, only the sound was so rich and other worldly that only the echo of it came to her human sensibility, and that didn't include ears. It felt more like petals falling from flowers on your skin only you could hear the sounds petals make when they're falling— so delicate, so beautiful—sweet music.

"All in all, I don't want to go back to visit that kind of meetin' again. The room was too close for me. I felt claustrophobic with so much going on at one time. And the people there seemed so sad and try so hard and are sometimes so mean to themselves, but not to other people.

"So many Christians are mean to themselves and not to other people. And they think because they are not mean to other people they are not mean, but they are mean to themselves. You don't beat anybody up, Miss Budge, not even yourself, though when you tell the truth some people who don't want to know what you think might think you are mean. But you aren't."

Mildred felt a kiss right then, just as sure as she was sitting in the chair. It landed on the back of her head right at the crown, melted into her scalp, turned into the essence of honey and flooded her brain before it went right to her forehead and eased the wrinkles there, pooled behind her eyes and softened her view of the world. That sweet expression of a celestial guardian's affection would permeate her being for the next several years of her life, pouring down through her heart to her toes where she stood with her feet shod in the gospel: the absolute and trustworthy truth that the Man had been born who came to fix what Adam broke. His name is Jesus. All of that happened while Mildred Budge was taking her next breath. Then Mildred said, "It takes a great deal of faith to love yourself in the name of Jesus." And then muttering almost to herself, the redeemed sinner confessed, "It's easier at times to love other people than yourself."

And in that instant, one aspect of both women flew away, and each instantly smiled at the other: Dixie-- whose face often wore a myriad of expressions, lost one of them— signified by just the tiniest of wrinkles disappearing above her left eyebrow. That presence of a personality broken by the past departed, and any name that might have been associated with it disappeared, too. Mildred Budge's face, long seen in the minds of children and their parents as the authority figure for learning and discipline, became more like the expression of the children that she had taught and still loved more and more all the time with the passing of every day—her capacity for loving others growing as her face lost the will to hold itself composed and dignified.

"The fellow who said the good-night prayer didn't use very many words, and it was more like he was telling God good-bye than anything else. His angel was holding a violin and began to play it right after the man prayed." Dixie stifled a wince. "It was not a very encouraging song. It sure wasn't a lullaby. It was more like a song you hear at a funeral. I hope I never hear it again," Dixie said, woefully.

"You don't ever have to go back to that meeting if you don't want to go. People were just trying to give you an idea of what behind-the-scenes church work is like. They were trying to be nice."

"We'll pray for them," Dixie promised. "Only my words won't be few."

"How many words are too many?" Mildred asked simply.

"If you don't say enough to keep that tall angel from playing that violin again you've stopped praying too soon."

16
PRAYING HANDS AND OTHER WAR STORIES

"I rotated off the missions committee so long ago I almost don't remember which chair I sat in, but I think it was the one by the back door cause I always try to sit where I can make the quickest escape," Georgina Wales said, after Mildred introduced herself one more time.

Mildred was taking her turn on the Helping Hands ministry of her church, delivering meals to homebound neighbors. Mildred had met Georgina several times before. The older woman remembered her; but Mildred Budge never believed other people would remember her, so she often re-introduced herself, giving others the idea that she might have a touch of dementia, but she didn't.

Mildred nodded that she knew the room where the missions committee met. She was no longer on the committee either— had moved on to the next outreach ministry, taking her turn doing this and that at church. The tin foil casserole dish she had brought to the ailing woman was still warm in her lap from the oven-- uncomfortably so.

"Do they still talk about mission trips and getting people to go so that they can experience the Call?" the woman asked, her eyes bright with curiosity. The eyes no longer had a color. They were watery with age but bright with gladness at having company and the prospect of warm food.

Mildred nodded; her stomach growled. Catering this woman's lunch had made her hungry.

The older woman waved a hand, pointing toward a stack of magazines. "You can set the pan down there. I'll get to it directly."

Mildred complied, glad to have the pan out of her lap, but noticed with dismay a drop of red sauce on her black polyester skirt. She didn't wear the skirt often—didn't know why she had that day looked in her closet and said, "Ah, my old black skirt." And then, wonder of wonders, after months of not eating ice cream and walking four miles daily, she had been able to get into the skirt with room to spare.

Georgina Wales was wearing an old baby-blue chenille robe. Her bony legs were covered in a pair of thick bright blue cotton pajama bottoms with white snowflakes on them. Instead of slippers, she wore yellow socks with non-skid tabs on the bottoms. It was summertime in Alabama, and Georgina had on wintertime pajamas.

'She is cold all year round,' the inner Mildred Budge chanted; and inside, where she hid her most secret self, the retired school teacher stifled a shiver of recognition and dread. Mildred got cold more often than she used to—was given to taking a light wrap to evening worship service now even in the summertime.

Mildred tamped down that shiver by taking inventory of the woman's state of being. Her poor old blue robe needed washing. A piece of dried elbow macaroni was clinging to the rolled collar. Her wiry eyebrows were mostly grey and shapeless.

"I guess I wouldn't know anyone on that missions committee now. I used to, when I was younger and beautiful and believed in romance."

The sentence hung in the air, a confession that defied the moment. Never easy with small talk, Mildred struggled to find an answer. Finally, an awkward silence later, Mildred said, "I've never been romantic."

A chortle sounded from the older woman, an odd sound of amusement that caused Mildred to jump. She pulled her shoulders back, straightening her posture, which was rounding with time.

"I saw that in you right away, or I wouldn't have said anything. Many women aren't romantic, as say some men are, but not many women will say it out loud. It has been my experience that men are far more romantic than women, and that is especially true about the work of missions inside the life of a church. I think people sense that it is a great, romantic adventure—and it can be—but it is more than that, and it is usually not a picnic."

"I wouldn't know about that," Mildred replied, primly.

"Oh, you do, too. You just don't want to say it aloud. You associate the question and the answer with gossiping or trouble-making. Telling the truth isn't gossiping, though it does sometimes cause some trouble. I'm just talking about facts that could have been included in the minutes of a meeting. Do they still talk about getting their numbers of participants up for the next mission trip, and do they still ask the question about why people are so apathetic about missions?" The woman's grasp of dynamics inside the ongoing work of missions was pointed, her voice growing stronger with inquiry though her colorless eyes did not change except to be lit up with a kind of delighted glee that did not fit the likely frustrations and helplessness of being in a wheel chair waiting on strangers to bring her a meal.

Mildred nodded instead, almost imperceptibly. It was a millisecond of agreement, of truth. Yes, yes, there was this perceived inertia in church life where missions work was concerned, and no one could really explain why. Or there was an explanation, and no one was willing to contradict the prevailing wisdom or traditions that had always been the business of missions. Maybe the season of planned missions' trips had run its course, and it was time to find a new way to reach out with the gospel.

The light in the room changed. Like the light in the wheelchair-bound woman's eyes, the light in the room grew brighter, warmer—friendlier. Mildred turned this way and that, looking for the light source, for the change was distinctive enough that it felt like a light had come on in a different room and had diffused its way to her--to them.

Mildred looked down at her plain unmanicured hands in her lap and then over at the hands of the woman in front of her, who had shaped and polished red nails and who steered her wheel chair slightly, turning automatically toward Mildred, coming closer until her feet were a few inches from Mildred. If her chair could have moved, Mildred would have pushed back, for the woman was now uncomfortably close to her.

Georgina saw Mildred looking at her hands and held up her fingers and wiggled them. "Big Apple Red," she said. "A lady from the Methodist church visits people like me and paints our nails. It's a sweet thing to do, isn't it? They call painting your nails a ministry, just like the kinds of ministries that the church supports formally as outreach. They call it being salt and light. It's funny about ministries at church. You can bake a cake at home, and it's called baking a cake at home. Bake a cake for some kind of social at church, and suddenly you have a cake-baking ministry, as if we can't do simple jobs without adding a title to it. People sure love titles."

Mildred nodded, tucking one of her own hands inside the other. She always meant to take better care of her fingernails but didn't remember to do it until someone else's well-tended hands reminded her.

"Is it mainly men on the missions committee?" Georgina asked, turning her head this way and that. Mildred thought she was looking for something she needed, only to realize that the woman had a crick in her neck and was trying to loosen it up.

Mildred smiled in agreement. "They are very nice men. I liked getting to know them. But the elders and deacons rotate on and off the committee the way regular church members like me do. We all come and go, taking our turns doing this and that."

The red polished nails reached behind her head, and Georgina rubbed her own stiff neck. "I miss men. Women come to see you. Most men usually don't," she confessed suddenly, warmly. "When you are younger they don't come to see you because they are afraid of moral failure. I heard that once from a preacher. Fear of moral failure. And then later in your life, they don't come see you because they don't want to come to see you. Moral failure of a different sort."

"I haven't thought about it," Mildred replied honestly. This time the other woman didn't contradict her. Mildred stole a glance at her wristwatch. Five minutes gone. Another fifteen minutes at least before she could tactfully make her exit with the truthful explanation, 'I have to deliver another disposable tin-foil pan with a casserole to someone. It's getting cold out there in my car.'

Georgina intercepted the time check and ignored it. She wanted to talk. "I miss men. I love the watchful-going-to-do-it-soon posture that is so much a part of a man who has been assigned guard duty at church—the elders and deacons—and sometimes a preacher. But men—men serving in church doing guard duty--they're precious. Just precious. Overall, I find men very good company indeed. That's why I miss them." The older woman grinned, but it wasn't lascivious or mournful. It was simply a grin. "Would you like to hear a secret?"

Mildred could not resist. "Yes, please. I love secrets."

"There is one man who comes and cuts my grass for me, and he won't tell me his name. He just cuts the grass, and then he comes inside and sits where you are sitting, and he brings two beers with him, and we each drink one. I don't really like beer, but he needs me to drink it with him, so I do. It's my beer-drinking ministry," she said with a wicked grin.

Mildred was thirsty enough in that moment to wish he were with them. "Who is he?"

"I don't know for sure. It's wonderful to have a gentleman caller who is unafraid to sweat, and who will sit with you and drink anything."

Intrigued, Mildred asked, "Surely you have asked him his name?"

"Surely I have," Georgina replied with another deep chortle. "But then I could tell he just wanted to be invisible like all of us are, so I didn't ask him a second time. You don't imagine that a man would ever want to be like one of us. Powerfully silent. Stealthily invisible. Free inside our quiet faith. Can you imagine? But he has asked me questions about all of us—what it's like to be invisible and unheard. What it's like to be done unto in the name of Jesus when we are old and set apart and seen only as old and as someone who needs things done to her and for her."

Mildred's face showed surprise, confusion.

"Like church ladies. What a great gift we have in so often being able to walk around invisible, and he wanted to understand our freedom. He's a very unusual man. We've talked about many things, some of them important. He's a good listener. He lets me talk. Like you."

The woman reached behind her head with her left hand and fiddled with the knot of grey wiry hair that was twisted there and pinned. It wasn't exactly a bun, and it wasn't a French twist. It was a knot of hair. "He asked me what it was like to be old and done unto with manicures and delivered meals, and I told him the truth. He listened. In missions they call these kinds of tender mercies—missions ministries-- building a context for the gospel being the fragrance of Christ. They have high hopes for building a context. I say declare the gospel and let the good news that Jesus saves build its own context, but nobody listens to me except him and you."

Mildred leaned forward attentively.

As if she were talking to the beer-drinking yardman instead of her church lady helper, Georgina continued, "Oh, my dear, people have good intentions throughout your life, and they do the best they can, but they are not all lovers and best friends. They are often passing shadows and phantoms—people coming and going just like I am, only I am doing it in this wheel chair."

"Bleak," Mildred replied.

"Freeing," Georgina said immediately, grinning.

Mildred waited.

The woman paused, a smile dancing in her colorless eyes and brimming on her face. "I have asked him what he does for a living, and he always says, 'I don't do anything. I just show up, and the Word does all the work. To celebrate my helplessness I drink a beer.' And then he holds up the bottle of beer and toasts the moment with me, and I nod, and I take a tiny, tiny sip of beer to keep him company in his announced helplessness. He leaves me and goes somewhere and gets dressed up, and I think he is a preacher, but he refuses to identify himself. 'Just call me the yardman. I'm here just helping you take care of your little God-assigned patch of Eden,' he said one time. "So I don't call him anything except yardman."

"Maybe he has a lawn business," Mildred suggested.

"Or he's with the CIA or in the witness protection program. Sometimes I like to think he's on the lam, and I'm aiding and abetting. I've got some sinner left in me. He could be anybody. Most of us are somebody other than who we look like to others. Who are you really?"

"A retired school teacher," Mildred answered immediately. It was her go-to answer, the stock-in-trade answer of social exchange.

The woman pressed both of her hands on the arms of her wheel chair and leaned her head back again. "That preacher takes off his shirt when he mows...."

"So you think he's a preacher?"

"Sure. He's got preacher written all over him. Only he's a preacher who wants to do some physical work. Can you imagine how tired he must get of standing in one place Sunday after Sunday trying to tell the truth without offending somebody who has a tendency to want to be offended?" she said. "My beer-drinking ministry is to let him mow my yard and then sit right here and not get offended by anything." And without letting Mildred steer the conversation to a safer subject the old woman repeated her question: "Who do you really think you are that you don't tell other people?"

"A bag of bones. Some hot air. Someone who comes and goes doing this and that," Mildred replied instantly, honestly. It was very freeing.

The light in the room grew brighter and brighter. "I love it when the light does that. Have you noticed?"

"Yes," Mildred said. The light revealed the room. A fine layer of dust covered all of the furniture. The carpet needed vacuuming. She wondered what the bathroom looked like.

"You haven't asked me who I am," Georgina prompted.

"All I know is that you are the lady assigned to me to take a meal to, and your name is Georgina. Georgina Wales," Mildred recited, suddenly a school girl taking a test.

"You're cute for an old broad," Georgina said, and then continued, "This bag of bones went to war a long time ago and learned the difference between being on a missions committee, being on a mission's trip, and fighting a war. Evangelism is war; missions at a church is more akin to a church picnic. It's romantic, but it doesn't inspire the kind of stories that will initiate the kind of action they crave. You can't really blame anyone for that. If people don't have the experience of a war to compare to the experience of a picnic they don't know how to think or say that. Some people in charge of community outreach efforts are gifted in administration and naturally believe that administrative frustrations are the same kind of event as spiritual warfare, but it's not the same. Am I offending you?" Georgina asked brightly, almost hopefully.

Mildred imagined for a moment that the older woman was trying to pick a small fight.

She deflected. "I've never been to war," Mildred interjected, oddly miffed to be described as cute, and surreptitiously stealing another glance at her watch. 'How rude would it be if she got up and found a cloth and dusted while they talked?' Dusting was real work. If she dusted, it could be called the ministry of dusting. If she didn't dust, it could be the ministry of not dusting. It took a great deal of will to stay seated when there were housekeeping tasks to be performed. 'What would it be like to have to sit in that chair unable to do one's own work?' Mildred inhaled slowly, and held her breath, moving into that composed inertia that looks like the ministry of apathy, but it was the Christian virtue of patience.

"My hands do most of my talking for me now," the older woman said. "I learned to let go of myself--to hold up my hands and let the breath of God pray through me this way. The first time it happened, it shocked the fool out of me, and I mean what I said. It's not just an expression."

Georgina stretched out her arms, the way preachers did when they were leading the congregation—when you are supposed to be sitting there with your eyes closed. Sometimes Mildred watched the preachers; and when she did, she never loved them more than when they were taking flight, their arms outstretched winglike, palms sweetly upward, their heads sometimes bowed—sometimes sunflower face up—and there had been more to that kind of praying than the ritual of public prayer. There had been this experience of ease and a present light which now had grown brighter in the room. The old woman had bones and flesh that trembled with wrinkles. Her flesh waved in the air, like flags in a breeze, and her head tilted back as sounds gurgled up out of her that were not words exactly.

And then it happened. A battle occurred and Mildred saw it: saw the battlefield, saw the panorama of time from beginning to end. There was Adam falling, clinging to Eve, and then came Abraham and a trail of children following him. Next were all sorts of men with titles that had the word prophet attached. Oh, my Goodness! She suddenly saw that prophets were more warriors than anything else. And then covering all of it was the Man on the Cross, his arms outstretched, owning space and creation, gathering and releasing all at once, his palms pierced, blood and mercy flooding the scene. Christ poured forth a peace that covered the whole universe and the ones beyond that and, simultaneously, managed time. He solved the problem of sin. Sin was real. So was peace. So was His invitation to be saved from ourselves and join Love and find Peace inside the Light of Life.

And then the old woman's hands lowered, and the vision dissolved—gone just like that. Mildred had never seen anything like that prayer before, and the sight shocked the fool out of her.

Mildred fought the urge to hurry over and hold up Georgina's arms for her, but the woman's eyes opened. Something in the gaze stopped Mildred from moving out of her seat where she was wearing a skirt. She never wore a skirt. You can't fight in a skirt. Mildred's fingers brushed absentmindedly at the drip of red sauce which would eventually dry enough to flake off.

The old woman laughed. It was a different laugh—a low rumbling of deep pleasure. "I had a taste to fight years ago. When I was on the missions committee and they were talking about setting up missions' trips so that someone could experience the Call, I thought it was so very romantic—so romantic. I guess they thought they were matchmakers. By then I had known warfare—the battlefield, you see. Family excursions or travelin' picnics weren't necessary for a woman like me. It was too quiet. God had already called me to fight---to fight hard. I developed a taste for fighting early on. I exulted in the hardscrabble rumble tumble of proclaiming the gospel right out loud with no excuses built in for not shouting it if people weren't listening or if others weren't ready to hear it yet. I had learned to fight, and in that room where the missions committee met I just couldn't sit still forever because I had a taste for battle. I didn't want picnic foods or polite, clean, indoor work. All of it was good work, just not the overt work of someone who was called to witness and to fight—fight to tell the good news anywhere I could to anyone who was hungry for Love. When people are hungry and thirsty for Love, they don't need much of a table set. They just need someone to point them toward the Bread and Water."

Mildred leaned forward, her hunger for lunch forgotten but a deeper hunger growing—one that had been there all along but was strengthening, searching, and inside the hunger there was one word repeating like a chant of unceasing worship, *yes, yes, yes.*

Georgina took a sip of water from a nearby glass heavily smudged with her fingerprints, and continued, "Like I said, I was never romantic."

"Me neither."

As if Mildred hadn't spoken, Georgina continued with a confession.

"I did have a romantic impulse not long ago. The other day I tried to send a message to a preacher I listen to on the radio sometimes. I had a do-gooder here who goes to his church, and she said she was going to see her preacher later in the afternoon, so I said, 'If you can work it into the conversation, tell that preacher that he keeps me company as often as I can remember to tune in to him on Sunday mornings. I think he's absolutely swell.' And she said she would if she could. I have tried to send him many messages like that, but I never know if he has ever heard them or if anyone has ever passed along the message. I listen to him preach Sunday mornings on the radio, and I think he's swell," she said, repeating herself.

A lot of people repeated themselves—younger and older. Mildred had learned from personal experience and from being on scores of committees and making visits that people repeated themselves often out of a need to be finally, finally heard. It wasn't always age or dementia. A lot of repetition in conversation came from a yearning to be heard, finally heard.

"You're curious, aren't you?" Georgina asked. "Curious about the light in this room?"

Mildred nodded, her hands growing jittery in her lap. A restlessness had been coming upon her from time to time—a fidgeting in the pew that she couldn't explain.

"People come to see me now bringing pans of food and casseroles, and some of them pray with me."

Before Mildred could offer to pray, the old, old woman waved a hand. "Ah, words in prayer. What a funny event words are. They are sweet, like men and women who fancy themselves wordsmiths or prayer warriors--"

"We say that at church a lot," Mildred mentioned, relieved to have something to say.

The woman threw back her head and let loose a keening wail, so sharp, so sudden, and so intense that Mildred sat back in her chair as if hit by a blast of tornadic wind. This old woman was given to fits of expression that didn't sound, in that moment, exactly human and certainly not romantic. There was absolutely nothing ladylike about her.

"I shall die, finally, one day. I do not seek it. I do not fear it. I sit in this chair in this accompanying light and grow older by the day and in ways that the young—that is you, my dear Mildred Budge—cannot fathom. I am at war still, fighting the great fight, keeping company with One who has taught me to pray the greatest prayer of my life and the One that brings life even as I'm dying here in what my yardman calls Eden. This is what I pray: 'Thy kingdom come. They will be done.' I don't have to go anywhere else to do it; but if I did need to be somewhere else, He who makes the travel plans for me would roll my chair in that direction. People like me never need a travel agent or a matchmaker," Georgina explained with an unapologetic grin.

"Oh," Mildred replied weakly, until that moment, one of the fine church ladies of the South but suddenly just a vapor, really, a bag o' bones and some hot air going here and there.

"Have you been in love?" Georgina asked suddenly. "It's none of my business, but my curiosity is not idle."

"Not recently," Mildred replied.

The old woman let the traces of her whole life pass across her face in sympathy. "This love—this devastating love affair with the Prince of Life—it will break your heart in ways that you didn't know your heart could suffer from time to time...." And then she leaned forward, her eyes bright with a stored youth. An eternal delight existed in the old woman that Mildred had never seen on any bride at any wedding in her whole life: "Love like this kills everything in you that is false and brings to life everything possible that is true. It doesn't break your heart for long. It stops your heart from time to time—you die, that is, along the way—and then the churning soul-breathing part of you is brought back to life remade. Yes, He remakes your heart until you are here, like this, and know what soldiers know when they come home from war and find that all is well on the home front after all. You are finally at home. Home. Finding your rightful home is a more powerful event than passion of the broken-hearted sort of which you speak."

"I didn't actually say brokenhearted," Mildred said, and her own thoughts diffused in that moment, moving in and out of time as this other woman's did. For a moment, the facts of their life stories were distinct, separate, but they were at one with being able to live all of their life in a single moment—a true moment of pain and hope.

The older woman waited until Mildred's thoughts refocused in the present, the very present, the verily, verily present, and then she spoke again. "It isn't anything to be ashamed of—living on as you have with a broken heart. And it is my suspicion that romance didn't break your heart. Seeing what people do to one another broke your heart—has broken your heart repeatedly," she said. Reading Mildred's face, the prophet continued: "You have seen people hurt each other and sometimes in the name of Jesus and in the name of missions, and your heart's been broken by what you saw. You don't tell people that because it hurts you so deeply to know it."

Tears did not come to Mildred's eyes. Her face grew impassive instead. Over time her features had been trained to obey her.

Georgina waved a hand airily, as if she were holding a kerchief like ladies of old. It was a strange hand movement to see in that small room where the light kept shifting. "Time passes. Wounds don't necessarily heal. Chronic pain can feed you if you understand that. Life goes on. Real life. Not images or idols that we want to call life. He happens. God happens to you. Jesus is real, and the Bible tells the truth about him."

"I read," Mildred said, to have something to say. She was growing more wordless by the moment, and inside a deep keening wail was getting born, such a wail of urgency that others were not paying attention. *Attention. Jesus is real, and the Bible tells the truth about him.*

"I got to where I just told people out in the field, 'Say His name, and watch what happens next. Come alive.' I told 'em, 'When you give up hidin' in the dark and say His name out right you come right on into the Light. You come alive! Being born again doesn't mean all the years that you lived before and called life before were wasted years. The lost dark years just make coming alive in the Light so much more intense.

"Just say yes to Life and Light—to the Bridegroom's unceasing proposal, and then never stop saying yes," the older woman said, talking to herself, talking to Mildred, talking to all the people she had ever talked to. "I do. I do. I do." Her words became a bride's chant she couldn't stop herself from saying. "I told 'em, 'Say yes to Him all the time, and you will learn it for yourself. Say yes to lightning and thunder and great rushings of Living Water and to rest and stillness too and to every moment of your life so filled with faith promises.' There are so many ways to say that last phrase."

Mildred nodded, dumbly.

"So what did you bring me in that tin pan over there?" Georgina asked companionably. The sleeve of her blue robe fell away, and her poor bruised arm was more purple than flesh-colored, scarred in so many places that it could have been a map of a foreign country. Maybe it was.

'Blood thinners did that to skin,' Mildred recalled.

"What the committee said you liked to eat. It's not much. Not fancy."

Georgia grinned. It was a jack 'o lantern smile. "Hand me a spoon, will you? I haven't eaten since yesterday."

Mildred went to the kitchen, where dishes were stacked to dry on a t-towel, and picked up a spoon. The kitchen was rarely if ever used, it seemed, except to wash up, and the few dishes used by the soldier in the other room were simply being recycled.

When Mildred returned, the woman answered the unasked questions: "The hospice lady washes up sometimes. And then there is a Meals on Wheels lady who brings me a meal sometimes, and she comes in and washes up, though she's not supposed to. Another person comes and helps me get a bath three times a week. On Saturdays they wash my hair. The Methodist lady manicures my hands but not my feet. I don't blame her. My feet are bad—real bad. There are times when no one comes, and I take a wash cloth and run it over my head and call that clean. After a while you learn to keep your eye on the door, your ear tuned to the earth and beyond, and eat in the here and now like this with a spoon." Georgina reached for the casserole dish, and Mildred moved and helped her position it in her lap.

Off went the tin foil cover, and the old woman grinned broadly. "I love baked beans," she said, spooning a large mouthful. The red sauce dribbled down her chin and onto her robe, landing near the dried-out piece of macaroni. Georgina was oblivious, eating one big spoonful after another. "Is there anything better than a good meal?" She asked Mildred, her eyes glowing colorless in ecstatic gratitude again.

"Dessert?" Mildred inquired innocently. She had an emergency bag of M & Ms she could leave behind if the woman liked M & Ms. It would be difficult to give them up because Mildred loved candy, but she was willing to make the sacrifice.

The old woman stopped eating, her spoon poised like a banner in the air, as she told Mildred Budge, "Oh, honey, I haven't wanted dessert in years."

17
MUFFINS ALL AROUND

"I guess you probably know why I'm here," the church lady said too loudly.

Preacherman was used to church ladies speaking too loudly at first when they came to visit. They were so unaccustomed to speaking in church that it took them a while to fit their voice to the surroundings. 'That, or she thought all men were hard of hearing.' Preacherman smiled encouragingly while the church lady looked around the office, apparently disoriented by a room that was decidedly masculine. He pointed toward the chair reserved for visitors.

"No. I don't know why you're here," he replied truthfully. Preacherman wondered if there were enough Kleenex left in the box. Usually when a woman showed up like this and assumed he knew what her problems were—and he rarely did—she would eventually cry. They didn't teach you how to handle crying women in seminary other than to say: "Keep the office door open!"

Preacherman had added tips through the years on handling crying women to his ever growing mental list about how to survive being a preacher. Lesson 101 in Crying Women: Don't sit beside them because they get clingy. Under no circumstances get physically reassuring; they get clingy. Be distantly sympathetic; the tears dry up faster. Have the clichés ready: 'This too shall pass. Growing older isn't for sissies. What doesn't kill you makes you stronger. Sometimes you have to think outside the box.' Under no circumstances say, 'God loves you, and I do too.' Never say that. A woman will talk herself into being in love with you for years after that, sit out in the congregation listening to your sermons dewy-eyed, and shake your hand too long after service. Her palms will be disturbingly hot.

The church lady drew a deep breath and said, her voice growing softer to fit the dimensions of the room, "I like that picture of a duck on the wall."

"It was here when I arrived," he said, but it was also his way of deflecting: 'Try not to let them make a personal connection. Be warmly impersonal. When shaking hands take only her fingertips.'

"I'm glad it's not a picture of Jesus," she said, attempting to get comfortable in the hard-back chair. "No one knows what he looked like. Not really."

"True," preacherman said, sitting back in his burgundy cushioned executive chair. His eyes surreptitiously found the clock. He had five more meetings that afternoon and a sermon to write.

"I'm here to talk about my funeral," she said, her voice growing stronger again.

He sat up straight immediately. Quickly he scanned his memory of names on the sick list. It was short this month. Not too many people seemed terminally ill.

"We were born dying," she mused aloud, and her blue-grey eyes wore a baleful quality. He wondered if she were on some kind of medication.

It seemed to preacherman that there was a depressed-by-medication look in her church lady eyes. Sometimes he thought the whole world was dopin' it. Life, that is.

"I guess a lot of people try to tell you how they want their funeral to go."

He nodded, almost imperceptibly. He did have these conversations from time to time, but they happened mostly in passing and were meant to be funny and possibly brave. "Sing that hymn at my funeral, will ya?" and then there was a self-conscious laugh. "If you don't, I'll never talk to you again." Preacherman never knew what to say when people threatened that. It was a risky business laughing when someone made a joke about dying—real risky. It could come back to bite you in more ways than one.

"I want you to have my funeral early in the morning, say, about 10 AM, and keep it very short. Choose songs that have an upbeat tempo, and don't let too many people talk about me behind my back."

He readied himself to laugh, believing that she was making a joke. But the expression in her eyes didn't change, so his didn't either.

"Will you talk about me or will the assistant pastor do the talking?"

"Do you want me to talk?" He asked carefully.

"Not much," she said. "It's not that I don't enjoy your sermons. I do. Most of them are fine. But if you lead my funeral, just keep it short and sweet. Tell them I was a Jesus girl-- that I enjoyed life as much as I was meant to. That's what I've decided sovereignty and predestination both mean. I had only one regret, but I couldn't fix it. So there. Just leave it at that. Then tell everyone to go have a nice brunch where they eat hot muffins. I like hot muffins. I would like for people to think about me when they eat a hot muffin. When my grandmother died, we had the funeral service early. Then we all went out for brunch. We laughed and cried about all the good old times and then ate hot muffins—blueberry, cherry, and banana walnut. Ma would have enjoyed that. Tell them to go enjoy themselves because people need permission to do that these days. They think they shouldn't for some reason."

Preacherman nodded assent, carefully. His neck hurt. One day he would have to seek surgery on his neck for years of making that preacher nod. It was a difficult nod to make—a neutral, non-judgmental, cool-as-a-cucumber preacherman nod. It had taken years to perfect it. Sometimes when he shaved in the morning he nodded to himself while he moved the razor around, removing the white foam that revealed the face he had grown older with—not the face of himself as a young man, which he had mistakenly believed would remain his countenance. Now, he wore a foreign face that emerged out of white foam and in dark shadows.

"Don't you need to make some notes?" she asked suddenly. "I mean, there are a lot of us. I don't want you getting me mixed up with someone else."

Like a waiter who had just taken a dinner order, preacherman summarized her funeral plans efficiently, his eyes showing no emotion and his voice almost a monotone: "Keep it short. Keep it early, about 10, depending on when the organist can play," he added, and the church lady nodded that she understood that there would be people to coordinate and that he couldn't promise ten o'clock on the dot. "Don't let too many people talk. The music should be happy. Tell them to go eat a hot muffin."

"That's right," she approved, and she smiled at him warmly. "You were actually listening to me. Jesus does that too, and you have a good memory."

"So far," he said, thinking she would rise and leave now. Planning her funeral was a task on her to-do list, and she could scratch it off and move on. Preacherman marveled that he didn't feel more concern about her funeral plan, but she was younger than she was old, though he could not guess her age. He had never been very good at that. He did suppose that he should inquire if her death, was, well, imminent. That was a hard question to ask.

"How is your health?" He inquired delicately. Preacherman leaned forward, resting one elbow on the desk, and his chin, just for a moment, on his curled palm.

She looked puzzled by the question, as if it did not fit the context of their conversation.

"Most of the time I say I'm fine. I do feel fine. Some days I feel very fine. I don't have any pain to speak of."

"Is there a concern about your health that I should know about? We have support groups."

She considered the question. "Support groups!" She barked. "Ya kiddin' me?"

"No," he replied evenly. "We have various groups of people with similar health issues who help one another navigate the physical and spiritual landscapes of their human condition."

"Are you alive?" she asked sharply. "Just when I thought we were getting along so well!"

"I think so," he said, sitting back in his chair. "Yes, I'm alive," he stated calmly, unoffended. He absolutely never allowed himself to appear offended to visitors.

"Do they have a support group for preachers who talk like you just talked? Did you actually say 'navigate the physical and spiritual landscapes of their human condition?'?"

He barked an imitation of her laugh. "Yes, I did say that. But it was because I had to proofread the church brochure so many times that the lingo which explains our support groups got stuck in my mind, and I recited it just now as if it were a Bible verse. I deeply apologize for quoting the brochure. It was a reflex only. And, no, before you ask, we don't have a support group for preachers here." Not many real friends either. A couple. Mostly he had long-standing acquaintances. Most people just wanted to see him as the preacherman. Everybody thought he should be smarter than he was. Nobody would understand some days he wanted to go outside and take off his shirt and mow the lawn and sweat without fear that someone passing by would have an opinion about his being half-naked outside for the world to see. That had happened to him early in his preaching career. He had mowed his lawn with his shirt off, and some of the ladies of the neighborhood had seen him bare-chested in his youth and reported the disturbing sight of their immodest preacher to the elders who monitored such situations.

The church lady ignored his moment of surprise and confusion, returning to his routine question that was really a step in the series of protocol questions he asked people when the conversation was in danger of veering off into a long-winded ramble from which it would not return.

"I'm not sure what you would call my human condition," she said finally.

"What does the doctor call it?"

"Lucky," she said. "Only I don't believe in luck."

"Of course not. Believers believe that God is in control."

"I had a near-death experience a while back. Since then death has been keeping me company. Friendly company. I mean, I'm not afraid of death, but I don't want to go today either."

The expression in his eyes did not change. "So your death is not imminent from a physical condition?"

"I wonder about that," she admitted. "I do take chances now that I didn't take before. I race through yellow lights. Before I would have slowed down and stopped at the light. Now, I press the pedal to the metal, and call out, "Hallelujah! Jesus saves!'"

Preacherman frowned, putting on his preacherman face when sin might be next on the list of protocol questions to discuss. "Could you be testing God?"

"How could anybody do that? It's been my experience that anytime a preacher thinks he might have to answer an unanswerable question he tries to ask a question like 'Could you be testing God' to get around it," she said, honestly. "And the answer is, no, I'm not baiting, testing, or challenging God in any way. I just don't stop myself like I used to. Except when I am with people—my family—I find myself retreating, backing away in my spirit until I am watching them, and I find myself thinking, 'You all would have gone on just fine without me if I had died,' and I think, 'They don't really need me. I am not essential to their well-being. They could go on.' It's a relief to know that. If something happened to one of them, it would kill a part of me, but the rest of me would go on."

"That's life," preacherman whispered. He forgot to nod.

"That's death," she said immediately. "A part of me turns toward it now in a way I never did before. I practice being dead more than I ever have before. Today, while I was practicing being dead I figured I'd plan my funeral—save you or someone else the trouble."

"You don't think of killing yourself do you?" he asked, leaning forward. He stifled a deep breath he wanted to take so she wouldn't see that this question was more than protocol. For a second, he was concerned. *How would he ever live with himself if someone who came to his office didn't get the help she needed and then killed herself?*

"I like living, but I saw death up close a while back, and it made me clean out my closets and get my house in order. That's why I've come here today. I didn't want to leave behind a messy life, and you will be busy the day I die, so why should you have to spend your time making decisions about my funeral, when fifteen minutes tops—that's all—then...."

"Muffins all around."

She laughed. "Muffins all around."

The church lady stood up then, and looked around his room a second time. The light in the room was subdued, cozy, eliciting confidences that would be kept.

"Where we are all going it's very bright and Jesus.....Jesus would like the picture of that duck, I think."

"Do you want me to mention Jesus at your funeral?" he called after her. It was a serious question—one of the most serious questions he ever asked anybody. The answer told him volumes. How many of the fifteen minutes of fame that she would experience at her funeral should be spent on telling Jesus' story or hers? Some people liked the gospel delivered at their funeral so that their stiff-necked and backslid friends and relatives could hear it.

She stood in the doorway and considered his question. "Tell them to live like you've already died—it's very freeing." She flashed him a grin, and waited--was waiting for something.

Preacherman replayed the conversation. The church lady had been dropping clues. Clues. She wanted him to understand her story the way she wanted the story of her life known. What had she said? *I have only one regret, but I couldn't fix it.*

He let his eyes smile, arresting her in the doorway. He wanted to call out loudly, 'I'm on your side! You can trust me!' But he said instead, "Do you want to tell me what that one regret is that you can't fix on the day of your funeral?"

She smiled broadly, a smile of thank you for listening to and hearing me, really. "I should have told the truth about Jesus more. He is real. The Bible tells the truth about him. Salvation is good. We all of us spend a lot of our lives practicing being dead or being afraid of dying or avoiding getting hurt, embarrassed, or of offending somebody. A lot of what troubles us doesn't need to trouble us. It isn't necessary to be afraid at all. Lord have mercy, Jesus! My only regret is that I should have told everybody about real living with Jesus while I could."

18

BONUS EXCERPT
MILDRED BUDGE IN
EMBANKMENT

As Sam's burgundy Buick broke through the lightweight road guard and crashed downward through heavy brush, church lady Mildred Budge knew she was not going to die.

Her life story did not pass before her eyes. She felt no panic.

Later, Miss Budge would wonder about that--wonder if she had missed some kind of heightened insight into the meaning of her life. And as a thoughtful person does as she ages, the retired public school teacher would almost regret that she had not been more deeply touched by a near-death experience. What would she have learned that might have informed the rest of her life and made it better?

But in that moment, Mildred Budge thought first only of the inconvenience of being stranded in a kudzu-filled ravine nowhere near the interstate because Sam Deerborn, the chairman of the pulpit committee, had wanted to take this narrow two-lane back road to their destination on a quiet Sunday morning when there weren't other travelers about.

The church lady thought, too, of missing the sermon hour of the young preacher who was the third candidate under consideration to replace their previous pastor and next on the list for the pulpit committee to visit. Finally, she grieved that the elastic in her left knee-high stocking had failed entirely. The stocking was now rolled down around her ankle fully, and it was going to be a nuisance all day long. Oddly, reaching toward that irritation of a collapsed stocking was the impulse Miss Budge fought against---not death.

When Sam's Buick finally smashed into the ground, Miss Budge did not see the big picture of life and how death informs the understanding of it. She saw a rabbit that woke up when the car slammed into the earth, and her eyes were open long enough for her to see it sprint away.

After the rabbit, Miss Budge saw that the three other people in the car were remarkably passive to have sailed over an embankment. They chugged through brush as the Buick's tires tried to find some traction to counteract the powerful pull of gravity.

When the nine-year old Buick crashed against a trio of drought-parched pine trees, bunching up the sun-faded hood and triggering the front seat airbags to expand while dried brown pine needles showered them, Mildred, perfectly peaceful inside of herself, shouted jubilantly, "Jesus saves!"

"We're all right, Budge," Jake Diamond said in response to Mildred's excited testimony.

Budge is what Jake called Mildred. Just Budge. Mildred liked it. It felt like a nickname, a term of real affection, rather than a misuse of her last name, which happened frequently. Mildred looked down at Jake's brown hand holding hers. She marveled that someone was holding her hand at all, and she knew a start of embarrassment at being caught holding hands with anyone in public. As the car gasped, belched, and the panel of lights on the blood-red dashboard blinked out totally, Budge squeezed Jake's hand and asked, "What in the world?"

It was an open-ended question with broader implications that would later require prayer for an answer. Like the use of her last name as a shorthand method of address, Mildred Budge's question, "What in the world?" expressed stupefaction and concern. It was one of her signature prayers to God when he moved in his famous mysterious ways and was a companion plea to her other frequently uttered prayers of "Have mercy," "Help me, Jesus," and the universal cry of unequivocal helplessness, "Lord, Lord, Lord."

"Sam?" Jake said. "Lizzy? You two okay up front?"

Sam's head and torso were covered by the white billowy airbag which had automatically inflated. He was snuffling. That is, Sam was breathing. Mildred thought the slow rise and fall of his shoulders represented more a sigh of relief than the deep inhalations of breath that come after a big surprise when adrenaline surges and then recedes.

In the passenger seat beside him, Liz's airbag had also inflated, and the serial widow was fighting it, punching it with her small, prissy fists.

Jake let go of Mildred's hand and reached out and solidly gripped Liz's left shoulder. "Steady, Elizabeth."

That was Jake Diamond.

When his door opened and Jake stepped out, the car shifted, not dramatically, but enough to indicate that not all four tires were firmly on the ground.

Mildred went very still as she waited for Sam to become himself again, because he was just breathing deeply there in the front seat, held in by his shoulder strap and the airbag. The passenger door creaked clumsily open, and Jake's brown hand navigated the surprisingly resilient airbag and unsnapped Liz's gray seatbelt. Unlike Liz's hands that were balled up in little fists ready to pummel an enemy, Jake's hand was outstretched and peaceful. His hand seemed to quiet the troubled atmosphere inside the car that was charged with residual fear and surprise. Jake eased the airbag away with his gentling hands and coaxed the pugilistic Liz to a place of stillness.

He has praying hands, Mildred observed. *Hands that speak to God of us.* The odd idea faded away as her senses took hold and brought her more and more to the moment inside the car where they were now altogether in a new way. They were survivors.

Mildred saw Liz's face captured in the mirror on the down-turned visor. The aging beauty queen's expression was one of torment and fear--not at all the perky, starry blue gaze she was famous for at church and which had successfully induced four different men to marry her, all of whom she had buried.

"Come on out of there, Lizzy," Jake said. He helped Liz to shift her legs out of the car.

While the other woman made her escape from the front seat and as her first foot touched the earth, Mildred could almost feel the ground beneath her own feet, and that feeling of imminent connection drew her more and more out of that heightened place where she was living, breathing, and still saying inside herself now: *Jesus saves. Jesus saves. Jesus saves.*

Mildred released her own seat belt, felt around for her brown leather Grace Kelly handbag on the floorboard, opened her own car door, and let herself out. Jake's eyes met Mildred's as he continued to prop up the pale Elizabeth. Liz had raccoon eyes from where the fresh mascara she had been applying in the car had smeared. The collapsed white airbag, so like a crumpled pillowcase that now needed to be washed, bore traces of Liz's mascara, too.

"Let's get her over there," Jake said quietly to Mildred, who was now listening to that interior voice that had stopped testifying and was now quietly narrating the story of her life to her while she lived it. It was a very comforting still small voice that sometimes she thought was only her inner Miss Budge, and sometimes she believed it was the eternal voice of Truth just keeping an accurate record of history being lived out in her: *You have been in an accident. Sam is hurt and seems to be out of it. Jake is helping Liz and has called her Lizzy and she hates that. You are still standing, although the elastic band in your hosiery has failed entirely, so don't buy that cheap brand again. You need to see about Sam because Jake is busy.*

"Budge, get a move on," Jake commanded. He caught Mildred's eyes, and she felt the word 'steady' though he did not say it to her, and Mildred was gratified, for Elizabeth Luckie was the type of woman who needed to hear that word of reassurance from a strong man, but Mildred Budge was not.

Retired fifth-grade school teacher Mildred Budge was a common-sense, faith-created church lady who could rise to any occasion. She looked at Jake wonderingly, her left hand gripping her brown handbag that she used year-round. She had given up changing out seasonal handbags years ago as a waste of energy. Now, she used one well-made handbag until it wore out; then, she threw it away. *Who cared if the color of her purse matched whatever outfit she was wearing?* Chin up and ready to march to safety, Budge said forthrightly in a voice that was unfamiliar to her own ears, "There was a deer."

"There was," Jake agreed, finally scooping up the wobbly Liz. "Budge, you need to get over there by that tree in case this car is going to blow up or catch on fire."

Mildred looked around while Jake shuttled Liz quickly to a place underneath a red tree. Mildred Budge had often felt the need to learn the names of trees, but she was tired; and when she was fatigued, proper nouns—and that included the names of trees—escaped her. When that happened, Mildred only identified trees by adjectives and colors. She stopped, a faint smile on her face as she listed the trees she now identified that way. There were weeping trees, and Christmas trees, and good-smelling trees, and dead trees, and unkempt trees that needed to be pruned, and today, there was this red tree toward which she needed to move. Budge looked down at her root-bound feet and tried to walk. She blinked at her feet hard as if they were separate entities that could be telepathically commanded to move.

Jake reappeared, put a strong arm around Mildred's waist, and said, "Come on, darlin'."

Mildred could not remember when anyone had last put an arm around her waist or held her hand, though many people in Montgomery, her hometown, call everyone darlin' because they couldn't remember proper names either. She wanted to tell Jake that he was not remembering the rules about how people treated an older church lady. Even church ladies didn't properly hug or kiss each other; they gave those lipstick-saving air kisses to which Miss Budge had not accustomed herself. Mildred thought air kisses—a pantomime of affection that church ladies inflicted on one another—when unavoidable, were one of the great humiliations of being alive. Air kisses told a terrible story of no one quite making a connection with you—just sort of pretending to while passing through your life. When Mildred Budge thought of air kisses, tears occasionally filled her brown eyes.

"You got out of the car, so your legs can work, and they will work. Move that left foot, Budge. Now move the right foot, Budge."

"Left. Right. Left. Right. Left. Right." And then Jake's arm was no longer around her, and Budge was standing beside the woozy Liz.

"Thank you," Mildred tried to tell Jake, but the words came out all rattled because in spite of the fact that she was the inimitable Miss Mildred Budge and truly believed that Jesus saved, her teeth were now chattering from shock.

19

SAM

Just before the airbag inflated, keeping him from breaking his nose on the steering wheel, Sam thought dismally: 'I have killed them. It's my fault. Belle has been telling me that my driving's not so good, and maybe she is right. Maybe I should have given up driving last month when I ran that "Stop" sign.'

And then, even though the airbag did its job, something in the moment that was akin to impact made Sam black out.

The other passengers assumed that Sam's blackout was due to the accident, but that was not true. Losing consciousness was an impulse that Sam had been fighting for some time. Going over the embankment simply gave the retired Air Force colonel an excuse to allow himself to slip finally into a state of not-knowing that had been attracting him for months, maybe years.

All the responsibilities that he had chosen to bear and all the work that made up Sam's to-do list reached a breaking point at the embankment, and Sam simply allowed whatever inner force there was that managed a man's consciousness to say, "Lights out, good buddy."

Sam blanked out. But not completely. There was a part of his consciousness that hovered inside of him, taking note of what was going on while his eyes were closed and his face was learning the contours of the airbag. It was taut and flexible at the same time. There were other people in the car, but the chairman of the pulpit committee was all alone up against the airbag, and he surrendered--no fight left in him.

It seemed perfectly natural to surrender to inertia while the car was airborne and turning the steering wheel a fruitless endeavor. Then, the car slammed against the ground, and Sam exulted in that moment of impact. Would liked to have relived it over and over again in the same way that when you're a kid on a roller coaster and a fast dip on the track makes you swallow your heart, you want to do it again. Sam wanted to hit the ground again and again, and surrender over and over again to the experience of smashing into the earth. The collision satisfied Sam, and he hid that satisfaction inside the airbag as the car rollicked hard. They came to a harsh stop against the trio of pines.

Sam felt Liz's fingernails claw his right thigh, but her hand departed quickly when the grabbing onto him did not stop the car from lurching or coming to that final neck-jerking slam against the pine trees that were so young that they really shouldn't have withstood the impact of the heavy car, but they did. Dry needles dusted the top of the car, and Sam thought for a second, *I just washed the Old Girl and now she's a mess.* He saw instantly that she was going to be past ever cleaning up again. Inside the airbag, a smile too big to emerge on his face showed up inside of him, deep, deep inside of Sam where he kept his grit and his will and the determination to keep going. The Old Girl was stopped, and now Sam could take a time-out from cleaning her up, keeping her up, and assorted other chores that were his daily lot. The smile inside of him yawned as his memory began to do the job of recording the story, but he was not taking note of the story he would tell; he was identifying those parts of the story that he would never tell anyone ever. Not even God. For inside himself in the deep well of his soul, Sam kept a separate book about himself, and it was the story of what he was really like that no one else knew and which he didn't pay much attention to because what's the point? Life was a mystery, and in many ways, Sam Deerborn, who presented himself as an open book to others, was a mystery to himself.

For Sam had experienced a deep satisfaction in crashing into the pine trees—as if a part of him had wanted to do it all his life. And it reminded him of the mailboxes that lined the sides of the streets in his quiet Southern neighborhood, and how often, when driving down a street, his hand had wanted to steer the car over and knock the mailboxes down like bowling pins one after another, only he never had. *Why would a man even think that?* Today, Sam had hurt his Old Girl, a car which had been a faithful vehicle and which was now, most certainly, going to be called *totaled.* The man others knew as Sam Deerborn, Belle's husband, was sobered by the event. Inside of himself, the other Sam was bemused and curious about what he might do next.

He would have to say good-bye to his Old Girl that had been dependable, and they did not make this shade of burgundy for automobiles any longer. It was such a respectable hue of red, and Sam thought it was so much more reliable a color than the cherry reds of cars painted for younger drivers and which seemed to fade faster in the sunlight. No, the burgundy resembled the deep resonating hue of a good leather rather than a painted tin can, and the Old Girl had mostly retained the depth of her color except for the hood, which had faded some. If Sam had believed in naming cars, he would have called her Ginny after a girl he had gone to school with and whom he had thought of marrying before he had met his Belle.

"Sam?"

Face buried against the airbag, Sam heard his name called. Heard the deep assuring tones of Jake Diamond and then Mildred Budge getting out of the car, and Sam had a vague sense of being sorry earlier that morning that he had been rude to Millie for bringing along that blue Igloo cooler that he had reluctantly stowed in the Old Girl's trunk.

He didn't understand why he had been so cross, for Sam loved Mildred Budge. He loved her in the way that people who are growing older together learn to love each other at church, where one's home life expands so that you are not only residing at your residence, you share a larger sense of family. The reminder of the size of this heaven-bound family was the local church on the corner. Sam and Mildred had been members of their church for years.

Sam decided in that first moment after the crash that he needed to apologize to Mildred about the blue Igloo. Make things right. He would just have to find the right moment.

Before Sam could plan what to say in his head and add it to the always present to-do list that was much longer than the stuff he wrote down on a sheet of lined yellow paper on a legal pad each morning, he heard Liz Luckie whimpering. That was good, because Sam had heard her cry like that at her husbands' funerals, and that meant she would be okay. All three other passengers were going to be all right, and he hadn't killed any of them except the Old Girl he had been driving. Sam inhaled, and listened to his breath come and go, come and go. One day it would go altogether, but until then, breathing was like walking. Take one more breath. Let it out. Put one foot in front of the other. That was life. One more step. One more breath. Over and over again. And now he had lost the Old Girl. Well, it was his personal loss, and Sam would handle it. He was a man, and he could handle whatever he had to face. Sam's hands still gripped the wheel hard. Needing to let go, Sam held on and it felt to him like his hands were fixed to everything, and he couldn't get loose.

That is how it felt to him at church, too. At Christ Church, Sam Deerborn was the go-to guy. The senior elder. When no one else could get a job done, good old Sam could. When no one else wanted to do a job, good old Sam would. And he hadn't really wanted to chair the pulpit committee, because he had learned from experience that the grief you got from the congregation for whoever you hired simply wasn't worth it. You couldn't please everybody no matter how hard you tried and no matter how many informal polls you took on fellowship night or how carefully worded the questionnaires were that got mailed out to the congregation to find out what they wanted their next preacher to be. It didn't matter how hard you worked or how smart you were or if there were fifty great guys applying for the job and you chose the very best man for the job, that man would not be good enough for everybody in a church as big as Christ Church. No, Sam Deerborn had not wanted to chair the pulpit committee again. Three times was enough already!

Still, as much as Sam said that he did not want to do it—be the go-to guy this time--he did not want to see the process fouled up and the church end up with a man they would have to keep at least three years (That was the decent time to keep someone if he wasn't working out). So, reluctantly, against his own better judgment, Sam agreed to form the pulpit search committee and chair it.

He placed the job advertisements in the right periodicals and then logged in the resumes by date, read them, identified the top three candidates in order to save everyone some time, and passed out copies of the resumes to the committee members. All he had left to do was take the committee members to hear the three men preach before they—the committee--voted to invite the right one to come and preach to the congregation, which would then collectively vote yea or nay. However, once a candidate was brought in for the show-and-tell Sunday morning service, it was considered a done deal. The congregation usually just rubber stamped the hiring selection by voting yea. If anyone disagreed or took that other bothersome position of abstaining from voting either way (Sam despised fence-sitters), Sam would call them up and explain that it was so much better if they could tell the chosen candidate who would be offered the job and who would always ask, "How strong was the vote?" that "We're behind you one hundred percent!"

The four-member pulpit committee had recently visited the churches of the other two men and heard them preach. Today they had been on their way to scout the third and final preacher.

So far, the committee was split two and two in favor of candidates one and two. Sam knew reasonably that there should have been a fifth committee member to break any tie, but carting five people around was awkward even in a big Buick. So Sam had settled on having only four members to comprise the committee, believing that his powers of persuasion would ultimately mitigate not having a tie-breaking fifth person on board. The two girls would vote with him at least.

There was still this last and youngest preacher who had made the cut and who could, if selected, be the right guy for the younger members of the congregation; but looking ahead, Sam couldn't see how the whole congregation would be able to get along with such a young man or keep up with Steev, who spelled his name with the two e's in the middle, and what was his last name? If Steev, with two e's in the middle, was half the guy he was described as being by his references, he could walk on water, and no man was that light on his feet. You had to read between the lines when you read references. Too much praise of a candidate from a current employer could mean that they were trying to run him off and getting him another job was their way to do it.

Sam Deerborn had lived a long time, and preachers were only human, like the people they were called to serve. He had tried to mentor as many of the preachers as he could, even old Joe, who was supposed to have retired years ago but kept coming back to fill in every time a preacher left. Sam believed he could have been more help to old Joe if that old preacher had been the kind of old dog who could learn a new trick, but Joe wasn't teachable. He had no ambition in him either. That was the biggest problem with Joe—no forward motion in him. That is what Sam had tried to explain to him, but Joe had just smiled and excused himself—said he could hear his mother calling--which was a funny thing for that old preacher to say. It was only a while after that when Sam realized that Joe's mother could not possibly have been alive, so the old guy was losing his marbles, too. Sam hoped that this last time was the very last time they would have to call Joe in to pinch-hit while a new preacher was being identified and called to lead Christ Church.

"Sam?"

He heard his name again, and there was no ignoring it this time.

"Sam?"

Jake opened the door and pushed the airbag away from Sam's face. Against his deepest will, Sam's eyes fluttered open, and he was surprised to see some blood on the airbag.

"Sam, snap to. We've got to take care of the ladies," Jake said.

A hand was placed on the back of his neck. The grip of Jake's hand steadied Sam, calling him to attention. Sam felt his seat belt unsnapped, and Jake tugged on his left arm.

"No reason to panic. Everyone's okay. And no gasoline is leaking," Jake reported. "I don't think she'll blow up. The car is sitting fine."

Sam wanted to say something, but there was blood running down his face and into his mouth; and when Sam opened his lips, he found that he didn't like the coppery taste at all.

20
JAKE

Jake saw it all happening from the backseat where he was sitting with Mildred Budge. They had tried to put him in the back with that woman who had killed four husbands; but thank God, Lizzy had announced that she got motion sick in the back seat, so she was up front with Sam and away from him. Boy, Lizzy had beaten the tar out of the inflated airbag with those little hands of hers, and Jake couldn't help wondering what else she had done with them. A woman just didn't become a serial widow without having done something with her hands. Jake Diamond did not have to think twice about it. He had decided to keep his distance from that one.

Yet, there she was—Liz Luckie--sitting in the front passenger seat, and here he was in the same car with the woman he had decided to avoid, and Sam and Budge and he might all be in harm's way just because the Lady of Death was on board. Hadn't they just flown off an embankment?

How in the world did Liz, a professional beneficiary of men's estates, get put on this real live search committee to find a pastor for real live people who believed in a real live God and a real live Jesus?

Already the Black Widow was a problem. Queen Elizabeth had liked that first guy that preached on grace, and Sam had agreed with her because Old Sam didn't want the rich widow to have an opinion by herself. Obviously, the second preacher was the better choice for their congregation, and Mildred Budge saw that right off, too. At present, it was two against two. Jake Diamond and Mildred Budge were new allies.

Jake had been on enough search committees at the local university where he worked to know how to assess the viability of candidates and to read between the lines of what they put on their resumes and what they didn't and what they emphasized about their missions and what they didn't see as part of their job description. But when you cut to the chase, that first guy preached grace, which meant he wasn't willing to preach Jesus front and center, and fifty-six year old Jake was too old not to want to hear Jesus preached front and center.

The second guy had mentioned Jesus seven times in his sermon. He had chosen John the Baptist for his focus. But if John the Baptist was the first sermon—could a sermon on Jesus be far behind? And so, automatically, ipso facto, Jake Diamond voted for John the Baptist—the second preacher, hoping for more of Jesus down the road, and Budge had agreed with Jake's choice, though she had not explained why. Jake had meant to ask her why, but he had not been able to talk alone with Mildred yet. Lizzy was always around, and Sam ran a tight meeting. Sam did not allow any time for just sitting and talking, which was a shame because sitting and talking was what people really needed to do.

You would have thought there might have been some time during the ride in the car for just talking about the candidates, but Sam had gotten them off to a bad start this morning by being irritated with Budge for bringing a cooler on a simple day trip. Sam would not allow the cooler in the car or any kind of eating, and Budge was a church lady that way. She couldn't help taking provisions with her. It was what some old-fashioned church ladies did.

But not what a church lady like Liz Luckie did.

When Sam said that about Budge's cooler, Lizzy had let her icy-blue eyes smile as if seeing Budge put down made her happy. Then, after Sam reluctantly stowed the cooler in his trunk and they had been assigned their places in the car, Budge had pretended to go to sleep in the back seat, but she wasn't really. It was just her way of tuning out Lizzy who was talking ninety miles to nothing in the front seat, and Sam was going, uh-huh, uh-huh, and then the deer leapt right in front of the car and, a split second later, they were sailing over the embankment.

It was strange being in the air. It felt like one of those dreams where you think you can fly, and Jake had thrilled to the weightlessness. Budge had, too, for her eyes had popped opened, and rather than fear death, Mildred Budge had worn an expression of a kind of surprised delight—you just never know with women.

Being a sensible man, Jake did wonder if they were going to die as the ground came at them, but he had a funny peace about the whole thing. He remembered the strangest bliss--that he didn't blame the deer or Sam, who had chosen this dumb route instead of taking the interstate. Jake didn't even mind so much that Lizzy was on the pulpit committee and was putting on eye make-up while they were about to crash. She wasn't much of a mystery to Jake. He knew her type. Liz was one of those women you had to pay attention to, and when you did, you would not see a deer before it was too late. She would cause you to lose your focus about so many other things. Only there were too many things that a man had to keep track of. Jake didn't see how any man with a real life would have the kind of time to give Liz what she needed. Her type would drain a real man dry. Steal his thoughts. Feed on his complete attention. Demand his life as proof of his love, if he let her. Knowing that, Jake resolved as they sailed over the embankment: `Don't court death, but you don't have to fear it. Remember this. Remember life. Remember what it feels like to sail out without holding any grudges against anyone. This is what living is supposed to be.'

It felt like flying did in a dream. It felt like heaven.

Over the embankment they all went, while Liz was applying extra mascara using the mirror in the dashboard visor and attempting to make eye contact with Jake in the backseat, as if he, a black man who had made a comfortable life for himself in a white man's world at the university and at the mostly white church near downtown Montgomery, would mess up his life or, more probably, shorten it, by swapping meaningful glances with not only a white woman but also with a white woman who had buried all her loving husbands.

Jake almost laughed out loud when Liz attempted to twinkle at him. Jake Diamond didn't have a death wish. If he had been sitting closer to Budge, he would have elbowed her, and said, 'Look there. Do you see that? Do you see The Liz making eyes at me? I don't want to die.'

But Budge was hugging her door, doing that 'I'm asleep thing' and fighting the urge to scratch some itch on her ankle. Her hand kept stretching almost involuntarily that way. And then the deer leapt, Sam swerved, they smacked the railing, a limb dragged across the car's roof, and as they sailed out over the embankment, Budge opened her eyes and her mouth made an O, and then, just as a rabbit leapt out of harm's way, she started testifying that Jesus saves! As the car arced groundwards, it was like there was no sense of danger for her, and that's one of the chief reasons Jake stayed calm. Everyone knew that Mildred Budge had common sense; and when she didn't panic, Jake Diamond didn't either.

21
LIZ

They weren't the same angels that circled overhead at the last funeral when they had buried Hugh Luckie, her fourth husband. They were a different group of angels, much smaller than angels were generally thought to be, and they were circling so fast overhead that at first Liz thought they were spokes in some kind of celestial wheel. As the car went over the embankment and then rocketed downward, the movement of the angels slowed to the point that Liz could make out their shapes, and the same question that had haunted her for the last four funerals arose out of a deep well of grief that no one who had not buried all of her husbands could understand: 'What in the world is happening to me?'

Almost as soon as she asked that question, she heard FussBudget say "Jesus saves" and then the same question she lived with when she saw the angels: "What in the world?" Liz was relieved by the idea that plain-as-vanilla Mildred Budge might be able to see what Liz had begun to see years ago after her first husband died. For Liz Luckie saw bunches of angels.

And when the angels started showing up like that, usually somebody died. Or just had.

Then, people blamed her.

People didn't say those words out loud. They just made faces about her behind her back. Liz saw those faces the same way she saw those crazy angels out of the corner of her eye. She hated those angels that swirled as flashes of light and hovered and haunted and dared her to try and build a life that they would tear down by simply taking away the one she loved every single time. She had been aware of the angels for a long time, but it wasn't until the death of Hugh Luckie that she put two and two together and got the answer that produced her newest question: 'Why are angels of death trailing me around?'

And having finally figured out what the angels were up to— coming to take away someone who loved her--Liz Luckie had decided that when she saw the angels again, she was going to fight them.

Liz pummeled the airbag, trying to get at the angels of death that had stolen her husbands from her, leaving her alone without a soul to help her fasten a simple necklace or tell her when she needed to touch up the roots of her hair. She couldn't see as well as she used to; and when you have been a beauty all your life and age robs you of your beauty in terrible stages, you don't want to look so closely at your face or the roots of your hair or your poor hands that even wearing plastic gloves while dishwashing couldn't stop from looking older.

Liz punched the airbag. Then, she reached over and clawed Sam on the leg for getting them all into this fix. Then, she caught a glimpse of herself in the visor's mirror and screamed because she had gotten so old, though she was still only sixty (she planned to stay only sixty for as long as she could pull it off). Liz missed being beautiful desperately.

She missed all of her husbands desperately.

And she desperately hated to see the flurry of angels, because that meant only one thing: Death.

But who was going to die this time?

One of them? All of them?

Did Mildred Budge know? That woman knew more than she usually told. Liz had tried to get Mildred to be a friend—had almost succeeded—but then there had been that unfortunate accident with Winston, Fran's sort-of boyfriend. Because Fran Applewhite was Mildred's best friend, FussBudget had chosen Fran over Liz, and Winston's falling off the ladder had not been her fault, but Liz was blamed for it anyway, like always. Right when they were about to become friends, Mildred Budge had pulled away from knowing Liz better. Later, when Liz had tried to talk to Mildred about what had happened, Liz didn't get much out of Mildred except that frank brown-eyed stare that would make an honest judge start confessing his trespasses. Mildred Budge was famous for that cow-eyed stare.

Feeling misunderstood and panicked, Liz prayed in the car just before it smashed into the ground and then crashed through bramble until the pine trees stopped them altogether: "God, don't let one of the men die today."

For the famous widow knew her reputation. She knew how other men and women saw her.

But her reputation had not been built solely upon her husbands all dying. Since her last funeral, Liz Luckie had been unlucky in Sunday school classes, too.

No Sunday school class could keep her.

Liz had gone from class to class at church trying to find a place where she could sit and listen to stories about God without causing a commotion, but she no sooner sat down than the man in charge began to talk directly to her in front of everyone. If there was a cross-referenced Bible verse to look up, any man in charge in any Sunday school class asked Liz to look it up. If there was a name to add to the prayer list on the white board, the man in charge handed Liz the marker and asked her to write that name on the white board. If the leader in charge told a joke, he turned to Liz and waited to see if she laughed. Liz was always extremely polite about laughing at men's jokes. When Liz exercised common courtesy, the women scowled, and the other men felt competition for her attention take root and begin to grow.

During the coffee hour, another man would try to tell her a different joke that was better than the one the teacher had told because men were competitive that way. There had been times when Liz Luckie tried to be rude instead—had not even smiled and even let her gaze go a little frosty (and that could actually backfire because sometimes a frosty woman can make a man's love grow hotter), but it was hard to act cold when a man was trying to please you. Before too long in any Sunday school class or during the fellowship coffee time, Liz Luckie was the center of the men's attention and the object of other women's contempt.

Liz Luckie was a man magnet. And she didn't want to be. She just wanted to go to Sunday school, sit down, and not feel lonely for as long as the class period lasted.

For Liz was not one of those women who could get used to being alone. Many women could. Liz saw the women who could live alone. They all sat together on the pews that had become known as the widows' pews, but Liz would not join them there. FussBudget sat there, although she had never been married. There were women like that who appeared to be widows, but really, they were mostly old-maid school teachers or retired librarians or government workers. Whatever their marital status, they were women who were content to be each other's company. Not Liz. Never Liz. She would never consent to that. Never.

Just thinking about it made Liz feel anxious and in a hurry. Life was going by pretty fast, and she couldn't take hold of it or catch up to it. She wondered how other people managed. Did they ever have that feeling of either running or being pushed by unknown forces? As the car hit the ground and the airbag slammed against her face and mashed wet mascara around her eyes, Liz Luckie repressed the question that slithered up in her consciousness from time to time: 'Was there a real devil other than one's own fearful nature, and if so, how could one get away from him? Maybe the devil's real name was Time.'

Liz was haunted by bands of misery-producing angels and tormenting questions that seemed to come from the devil. She was scared.

Liz felt pursued by death, and she wanted to feel at peace with life in Jesus. Even last week she had been chased into church by old Mr. Peavy who had called out to her to slow down as she climbed the steps of the church. Only he didn't say those words, "Slow down." Mr. Peavy said, "Don't you look pretty?"

Liz had always been able to translate men's language, and she had known that Lem Peavy was asking her to slow down and walk into the church with him. And if they had walked into the church together, they would naturally sit together during the service. Then, he would hold the red hymnal for the both of them, and once she was singing the same song with him off of his page, well, she was done for.

That is how a courtship could begin—as simple as that. But this time, the question, "Don't you look pretty?' did not trap her. Because Mr. Peavy walked slowly and with a cane, she had been able to scoot away, moving right to the threshold of the church where the two deacons handed out the order of service. On the threshold that led to the sanctuary Liz had looked to her right where the widows' pews were and knew she would be safe there. It was a no-man zone, and Mr. Peavy wouldn't follow her there and sit down beside her. Still, as safe as it appeared to be in one respect, it felt dangerous in another. Liz simply could not join the other single ladies in the unofficial widows' section who announced their aloneness like that. She never had been able to join women who seemed resigned to being alone or old.

They were the type who wore those red and purple hats as if bright colors made up for living alone. Liz had a great deal to say about the ways that others duped women into wearing uniforms that made them all alike--even that purple and red combo meant to suggest independence and flair and which was just another uniform after all. Liz Luckie was herself. She was herself, alone now, and determined to be herself, alone now.

With that purpose in her heart, Liz had used her charms to inveigle her way onto the pulpit committee so that other people would see her as someone who didn't just get married and bury the poor man who had found her desirable. She was someone who had a job to do at church. She was going to prove it. She was going to help them find the right man for the job and not marry the man or later ask him to perform a marriage ceremony for her!

Liz was working on her reputation all right. She had been making progress, but there were those angels of death circling overhead again like buzzards in white, and she knew what they meant. God help her and the people who were in the car with her whose lives were in danger now.

'My Lord,' she began. Almost as soon as she thought the prayer, Jake's strong arms scooped her up, and like a groom carrying his bride, that man delivered her to safety, leaving FussBudget Budge to fend for herself.

Liz automatically closed her eyes to absorb Jake's strength. It was the same way she had always been carried by each one of her grooms except Hugh, her last husband who had died only four months ago. As a low humming sound began inside of her sounding like an echo of the wedding march, Liz forgot her intentions to be herself alone and allowed the smile of delight to surface that so many men had found irresistible.

But when Jake lowered her to the ground, he did not stop to receive the glow of her feminine approval. As her hero walked back to get FussBudget, she whimpered in a new assault of grief. Tears rolled down Liz's face, for Jake Diamond was immune to her femininity.

"See there?" she called out to the angels of death; and to her surprise, they zipped away.

22
MILDRED

Mildred continued standing unsteadily, her brown leather Grace Kelly handbag gripped tightly in front of her. Her brown slacks still looked pretty good. Brown didn't show dirt. Her aqua double-knit sweater felt oddly damp. *Southern women don't sweat; they perspire.* She plucked at the cloth to loosen it from her skin, where it wanted to stick.

"Did you all see a deer?" Sam asked quietly when he joined her and Liz underneath the red tree. He had removed his suit coat to drive, and so he was standing in his grey slacks and a white dress shirt. A few drops of blood had landed on his shoulder. He kept squinting, as if the sun hurt his eyes, but it wasn't only the sun. A continuous trickle of blood from a wound on his forehead oozed. He brushed at the blood as if it were a mosquito.

"I saw the deer," Jake said, pivoting slowly.

Mildred read his mind: 'Where are we?'

High above them, traffic could be passing by, but there had been no one else on the road that morning. It was a steep incline, a far way up. Mildred shaded her eyes and shook her head. Jake saw and nodded, almost imperceptibly. He turned toward a stand of trees to the west and considered it.

"I saw the deer, too," Mildred replied. The words rattled out of her mouth. She hugged herself, trying to still the shaking that wanted to rise up and claim her. *God, I feel cold, but it's warm out here. Help me.*

Liz had been putting on mascara and had not seen the deer. She quickly nodded, yes, quite vigorously that she had seen the guilty deer that had caused this problem only she was lying, and that small trespass against the nature of her God-given soul layered upon other small nods of the head when she had affirmed or denied something that she did not know to be the truth or not the truth. Unaware of having gained a kind of weight in that moment from lying casually about so many things, Liz kept staring at the sky.

The speed of angels was faster than almost anything else she knew. They could come and go in a cluster in the blink of an eye. Sometimes, she could feel them flying away, even though she had missed their approach—but she could feel their tailwind, the sudden rush of air as they whooshed off, headed to some other place where they had some kind of job to perform. There had been times when Liz had felt that whoosh and wondered, almost hopefully, if there were other women---and maybe men—who were aware of the angels of death. She would have liked to have met at least one other person who could truthfully say just as each one had confirmed to seeing the deer, "Yes. I know the angels you are talking about." But the widows and widowers at Christ Church would never fall into a conversation like that with her. Besides, most people blamed Liz for the appearance of death; and if she claimed to see angels about the time that death happened, they would smiled condescendingly, nod knowingly, and whisper. Whisper. Whisper. That's why Liz did not point when she saw them again. The angels—maybe twenty of them or more-- were now hovering at the horizon, a swirl of white that most people assumed was a distant cloud.

Sam took one look at Liz's concerned expression and knew that in spite of his head wound, he needed to take charge. Someone had to get the group organized. There had been an accident, but life can't be allowed to just happen to you. You have to make a plan, stick to the plan, and control the fall-out when something unexpected happens like this derailment from the schedule that had taken them over an embankment. Sam fought a wave of weakness and the strange desire to lie down on the ground and close his eyes. His mouth opened and words came, like the small trickle of blood that still flowed from his eyebrow where he had bashed it on the steering wheel, "Let's get organized. First things first--we need a latrine."

Sam didn't wait for anyone to agree or disagree. Scanning the options, he pointed with his left hand. "How about over there—behind those bushes? And water. I'll look for water, although we don't have a way to transport it." His face grew almost angry, and he clenched his teeth. "Water could be a problem."

Mildred raised her hand, like a student in school. "Sam, you're bleeding."

Sam yanked from his back pocket an old-fashioned white handkerchief that his wife Belle had monogrammed for him and stanched the blood drizzling from his eyebrow. He was glad for the wound, relieved that he was paying a steeper price for the accident than what the others apparently had experienced. No one else was bleeding.

Liz had ruined her make-up.

Sam squinted hard at Mildred, and he couldn't see anything wrong with Mildred except occasionally her teeth chattered.

And Jake—Jake was all right.

"It is too late in the year for berries, I think, but there might be a pecan tree around, though the nuts won't be edible this time of year. If we can find the right kind of water supply, there might be fish. And I think I saw a rabbit when we landed."

Almost immediately Sam realized that mentioning the rabbit was a mistake, for the skittering of the rabbit had happened when the car hit the ground, a split second before the airbag expanded large enough to obscure the view.

Mildred's eyes had been closed. Jake had seen the deer and the rabbit, but he had forgotten about the rabbit until then.

Liz had seen only her left eye in the visor mirror because she was dolling up. She was a pretty woman, and that is what pretty women did. (He didn't know why other women resented her for it.) Sam, who had supposedly been rendered unconscious by the impact, remembered seeing a rabbit, and he shouldn't have, really, because when you black out like that there is a cloud of amnesia that blocks out certain details of that moment of shutting down.

Only Sam remembered the rabbit, and he had stupidly said so out loud. It was a crack in the story of what had happened to them all that morning, and the crack made him want to sit down and hold his head in his hands and cry like a school boy. Instead, Sam clapped his hands together vigorously and asked, "Is everyone holding up okay?"

He scanned faces. Jake, Liz, and Mildred nodded solemnly.

"Are you all right, Sam?" Mildred asked quietly.

The older man pressed the handkerchief to his forehead again. The bleeding had eased, and there was now that crusty beginning of coagulation that would lead to healing later.

"No time to worry about me. We have got to get ready to spend some time here. Maybe the night." Though the news was unpleasant, something ignited in Sam's eyes, and both Mildred and Liz thought simultaneously: *This old Boy Scout wants to camp out all night and brave the elements.* Then, almost immediately, the two women's reactions split and went in different directions.

Mildred wondered why Sam wanted to stay outdoors overnight without the comforts of indoor plumbing and homemade food. And his wife Belle was at home, and she was not so well these days and might need him. *Why didn't Sam want to get home to Belle?*

Liz thought, 'Thank God! A real man!' Something inside of her that had been tied in a knot since her last husband's funeral began to unkink, and she felt, inexplicably, almost giddy. Still seated on the ground underneath the red tree, Liz leaned back against the trunk and exhaled. She didn't have to go home right away to an empty house. She could stay right there with two real men: one had carried her in his arms, and the other was now in charge.

Mildred waved her hand at Sam for his attention. He looked momentarily impatient that she had something else to say. "It is going to be all right, Mildred. When we don't show up at the church, the news will get back to the home front that we have gone missing. They will come looking for us."

"It could be six o'clock tonight or later before anyone realizes we're missing," Jake said.

Sam turned on Jake angrily. This was no time to upset the ladies. A man had to look on the bright side when ladies were around. Sam forced himself to speak slowly. "The young man we were going to see today will realize that we are not there."

"But that doesn't mean Steev will call anyone," Jake responded thoughtfully. "It just means he will think we didn't come. Or, that we got the date wrong."

"No," Sam said. "I told him we would take him to lunch afterwards so we could interview him. It's a rare young preacher who doesn't enjoy a free lunch." Sam attempted a short laugh at his own humor. It was a familiar barking sound that attempted to prove to everyone that he was jovial and good tempered.

Mildred flinched. For some time Sam's false laugh had felt like a stab in her heart. She could only imagine how his wife Belle felt when she heard it.

Liz studied Sam, taking deep breaths of relief that someone was in charge of her life.

"That was definite?" Jake affirmed, oblivious to the implications of that false laugh.

Something passed behind Sam's eyes. Not anger this time. Doubt. "I think so." He paused, and then remembered the ladies needed him to be right. "Yes, of course, it was definite."

Liz smiled faintly, a contentment growing in her. She had seen the angels, and no one had died. In fact, they had flown away. Maybe they were gone for good now. The Bible said there were seasons of things, and maybe the season of death's angels had finally passed away. Maybe they would never come back. Sam was becoming himself again. They would be rescued. In the meantime, Liz didn't have to stay in her dark, too-quiet house waiting for the phone to ring. It rarely did except when the politicians put their commercials on speed dial and impersonated real callers. But in that moment, Liz Luckie didn't have to listen to the politicians over and over again for company or try and read her Bible and pray, which was hard for her. She had never had the knack of doing that quiet-time stuff that everyone talked about at church. The quiet scared Liz. There was plenty of time to be quiet in the grave, and Liz was alive.

In that moment, Liz Luckie felt more alive than she had in months. Two men were in charge. FussBudget Budge was about to remind everyone that she had brought her big, fat blue Igloo cooler. It was in the car trunk where she had stowed it this morning. Sam didn't remember it. But FussBudget and Jake did. Only they were letting Sam have his head for a while so he could feel better about running off the side of the road— a simple country road, and not some major thoroughfare which the State Troopers patrolled regularly. They were out here in the boondocks. Liz smiled inside herself, thinking about how Mildred was standing there thinking she was about to save the day. That's what church ladies believed was their calling in the church and why they carried all that stuff in their church lady purses and had those Kleenexes tucked neatly up their church lady sleeves. Mildred and other church ladies like her were the kind of women who never understood what men actually really liked. But Liz did. Men liked to be the ones who saved the day.

"Sam?" Mildred said.

Sam was scanning the depth of the incline from where they were up to the top of the hill where the road curved, but there was no sound of other cars. None at all. And even if someone drove by, their car windows would be rolled up with the air conditioning going full blast. No one would hear them calling out.

"Someone could see the broken railing and call it in. Or a State Trooper might drive by and see it," Sam theorized.

"Sam?" Mildred said.

He turned to her reluctantly.

"Didn't anyone bring a cell phone?" Mildred asked.

23
ABOUT THE AUTHOR

Daphne lives and writes in Montgomery, Alabama. She is the happy aunt of several children including Jon Michael Linna and his sister Roxanne Nicole Linna, who told her very sternly to put her name in a book. It is their sweet faces you see on the cover of this book instead of the author's to remind everyone who is concerned with the Great Commission that the work of missions is for all the children of God, whatever their ages.

Other books by Daphne Simpkins
  Christmas in Fountain City
  What Al Left Behind
  A Cookbook for Katie
  Mildred Budge in Embankment
  Mildred Budge in Cloverdale
  Miss Budge in Love
  Nat King Cole: An Unforgettable Life of Music
  Coming soon: The third Mildred Budge novel, *The Bride's Room*

24
ACKNOWLEDGEMENTS

Friends encouraged me to share the gospel this way, and one of them helped to read and proof versions of the stories. She also shares the gospel on a regular basis as a teacher in the Berean Sunday School class. She's the best teacher I've ever had. Thank you, Guin Nance, for teaching, listening, reading, praying, and saying, "Try that again." You have been saying those words to me for a long time, and I appreciate your helping me learn to write. Keep painting.

Thanks also to Jon Linna and Lola McCord who generously let me publish the picture of their children Roxanne and Jon Linna on the book's back cover. Thanks also to Katie Thompson Photography for the beautiful picture.

Special thanks to my cousin Cecelia Murphree who always offers me words of encouragement about my books. I deeply appreciate your generous encouragement, Cecelia. Thank you.

And heartfelt gratitude to my dear cousin Kevin Scott Morris who lets me invade his house when I need to run away from myself. I hide out with Kevin from time to time, and he gives me coffee or sweet tea, whichever cure is needed. He also offers humor-rich advice on how to grow older in the South. Thanks for the laughs and for keeping me company, Kevin.

I have a lot of church lady friends, and while this is a work of fiction, the goodness of my friends often inspires me to celebrate that perseverance and kindness that is so much a part of church ladies lit up with the Light of Christ. I am grateful for the friendship of Lori Tennimon, Jennie Polk, and Sue Luckey. And to the patient Mrs. Asbury, you will be receiving a copy of this book from me with the following inscription: "For Joyce Kelley Asbury with gratitude for your kind interest in my stories and encouragement of my work." Much love to you all!

While the fictional Mildred Budge is still an active member of her Berean Sunday School class I, her biographer, have moved sideways to help lead discussions in the Barnabas Sunday School class where I learn more than I teach. Week after week a group of beautiful friends help me to read the Bible with purpose, prayer, and hope that we can grow in understanding and love under the authority of the truths of the Bible. Special thanks to our class leader Gail Clements who keeps the Barnabas class organized with her hospitable spirit and to Cam Fox for so often generously being the voice of experienced wisdom and encouragement which all of us need. Thank you!

And thank you for reading this book.

Mildred Budge and I appreciate the gift of your time.

Made in the USA
Monee, IL
05 September 2022

13282275R00108